Erotica Sex Stories for Women

Naughty Erotic Sexy Short Stories Compilation, Forbidden Menage MFM Harem, Adults Short Women Romance And More.

Sasha Coleman

COPYRIGHT

Contents

The gray shirt

The boys from my favorite football club were guests in the city for the cup game and spent the night in our hotel. After their fully deserved victory, they celebrated in the hotel bar.

In the meantime it was 1:30, only the hard core consisting of 7 men was still present. For me, this time meant one thing above all: after work. The boys regretted that.

"Oh come on, stay still!" Kevin. I would be smooth if Sonja gave me ok for that - which I doubted. I told him so. A determined expression crept onto his face.

"Anna , we have not yet toasted this grand victory with you! " Markus.

We already had, only Coke had been in my glass. That probably didn't count for him.

"You promised me another dance." Sebastian. I actually did, but I never thought that he and especially me would remember it. Which didn't mean that I wasn't in favor.

I looked briefly at the colleague and saw her nod.

I quickly pulled vest and tie and laid it on my things.

As soon as I had come out from behind the counter, I found myself in strong arms again.

"How does it look now out, young lady, dance anyone?" I heard Sebastian's rough Voice on my ear.

I swallowed, I hadn't expected that close. I quickly caught myself.

Who would say no? Certainly not me. So I hurried to nod.

Sebastian led me to the improvised dance floor in the middle of the bar under the cheers and whistles of the others, put his right hand under my shoulder blade as it should, but pulled me so close that maybe one hand fit between us would have.

Whoa!

Suddenly the beginning bars of a song I knew very well ran. Matt Morris - Let Me.

I looked confused from our DJ Michael, who just winked at me, to Sebastian. He didn't seem surprised at all, just looked at me intently.

Ookay ... what would this be? Why a slow song? Was Sebastian aware of the text of the song ?! Did he drink too much? No, he hadn't ... He had hardly had anything.

"Seb ..." I started to protest.

"Shh, just let me guide you. Just let yourself fall. ", He whispered calmly. His slightly scratchy voice gave me violent goose bumps.

The next moment he moved. It took me a moment to understand his steps, recognized a rumba. Then I turned my head off and enjoyed it was lying in the arms of this man who smelled so good, who led so wonderfully safely, who obviously knew exactly what he was doing.

I completely ignored the fact that there were other people in the room. I just didn't care if that would talk later. This was a unique opportunity that I didn't intend to give away. Sebastian would know what he was doing.

I put my head on his shoulder, which was at eye level. His hand on my back slipped lower and I felt through the thin blouse how he stroked my thumb with my back. When the song came to an end I wanted to let go of him again, but he didn't loosen his grip.

I raised my head again, looked into his blue eyes, which had darkened, however, and frowned in confusion.

"Another one?" He asked softly, insistently.

I would be the last one to protest.

A new song started seamlessly, slowly again, but more rhythmically.

Dean Martin - Sway.

With a jerk Sebastian started to lead me again. This rumba had a different dynamic, was more passionate than the one before. I noticed that at the latest when there was no leaf to fit between us and we touched all over our bodies. One of his legs slipped between mine, causing one of mine to be between his. His torso radiated a heat that I felt almost unfiltered through his shirt and blouse.

Unlike before, I couldn't get rid of his eyes, almost lost myself in it. His eyes were fiery and went to my core. I had the feeling that he could look into my soul, read me like a book.

When I felt his middle rub against mine, I gasped and the little triumphant smile that played around the corners of my mouth spoke volumes. In the course of the dance we rubbed each other lightly again and again and I felt that that didn't leave him cold either.

I was wax in his hands and we both knew it.

"Come on, let's get out of here," he said when the song ended and he released me.

We sat down at one of the high tables and I looked at the counter, slightly dazed, saw Sonja looking at me worriedly. I smiled at her. Everything was fine, I knew what I was doing, but she raised her eyebrows nonetheless,

my gaze went on and met 6 grinning faces.

To Sebastian I said: "Not together. Where do you live? I'll be right there. "

He sighed but nodded." Very well. I've got the 521. I'm waiting for you. " He stroked my waist.

He got up and left the bar without turning back to his boys, who called out some rough comments afterwards. I grinned furtively.

I went behind the counter to get my things.

"Anna, will you come with me for a minute?" Said Sonja in a tone that did not tolerate a contradiction.

I followed her into the next room and listened to what she had to say.

"Listen, I know you're old enough, but are you sure you want to? And are you aware of the consequences? Anna, when that comes out. I don't want you to regret that in a few hours. You are otherwise so sensible! Be aware that this is most likely a one-time thing for him. Do you want to risk your apprenticeship for this? "However, she seemed to know that she was just falling on deaf ears with me.

" ... Anyway, I'm here for you, okay? "

"I ... thank you," I smiled. That was exactly the problem. I was fed up with always being sensible, always doing the right thing. It was still good to know that you have colleagues like that. And Sonja was trustworthy. "I know what I'm doing. But, please, don't betray me."

"Well then ... I wish you a nice rest of the evening.", She sighed.

"Thank you," I grinned and hurried to get out of the bar. I took a quick detour to the staff changing rooms and freshened up before heading to Sebastian's room.

I took a deep breath in and out of his door before knocking softly.

It only took a few seconds before he opened the door for me and quickly pulled me into his room.

He closed the door and gently pushed me against it. My hands went up the back of his neck while his left was on my neck and his right was lightly massaging my hip.

His face came dangerously close to mine and it was like in the bar again when we just stared at each other. It was then that I realized that I wanted this, that I would live with the consequences if there were any.

"You're driving me so crazy," he whispered roughly and then closed my lips with his.

Slowly, he stroked his lips over and over until he ran his tongue over at some point. I opened myself too readily to him and came to his tongue with mine. At first they circled lazily, but soon the kiss gained passion and we fought a sweet fight.

We breathed away from each other after what felt like an eternity and I felt his hot, fast breath on my cheek. Shortly thereafter his soft lips were on my jaw, teeth brushed my earlobe lightly, made me gasp softly before he sucked lightly on my lymph node. This elicited a short moan and I clawed my hands in the back of his head.

He continued to kiss down on my larynx. I put my head back as he slipped his hand from my hip to my back and slipped under my blouse. His fingers were cool on my heated skin and I shook myself slightly. In the meantime he kissed and sucked on my collarbone, always eliciting small lusty sounds from me.

Suddenly I felt his thigh rub against my middle.

"Basti," I gasped. The friction triggered a wave of excitement, my heart beat faster, my breathing became deeper, and my lower abdomen pounded comfortably.

I ran my hands under his shirt, explored his torso. So when I drove over his abdominal muscles, I didn't notice with satisfaction how they tensed. I couldn't wait to see him without a shirt. My fingers moved further north, brushing his nipples. Apparently he was very sensitive here because they hardened immediately and he gasped. His fingertips danced over my back and ran lightly down my spine. I pushed my back through and pressed close to him. He took over my lips again, this time it was a hard, quick kiss that left my lips tingling and swollen.

Sebastian grabbed my hip and started walking backwards towards the bed. When our legs hit the bed frame, he dropped on it and pulled me with him so that I landed on it. He pulled me down to give me a tender kiss.

In our case, his shirt had also slipped up a bit, so that his well-trained, slightly tanned stomach was now revealed. I put my hands on the hem of his shirt and slowly pushed it up, running my fingertips over his warm, soft skin.

He straightened up a bit so I could take it off completely and I carelessly dropped it on the floor. I looked at him before I started to explore his torso extensively with my lips and fingers. Especially when I devoted myself to his nipples, I not only heard how much he liked it, I also felt it clearly on my thigh. He pulled me up a little to kiss me. Again it was passionate and demanding and I couldn't get enough of his kisses.

As he pillaged my mouth, I felt how suddenly I could breathe more freely. I lifted my head in confusion to see why. Sebastian had opened my blouse and was now looking at me closely. I took off my blouse completely and dropped it to his shirt.

When the cool air hit me in the room, goose bumps spread over my upper body.

"Cold?" Sebastian asked and started to sit up. When I realized that I was still lying on top of him, I stepped aside.

His eyes went hungry again over my upper body and he reached out to follow the approach of my breasts above the bra. His thumb went into the cup and stroked my nipple lightly. I involuntarily closed my eyes, felt the wart harden and straighten up, and gasped softly. He repeated the movement a few times, stroking it and circling it. Each of his touches seemed to increase my excitement. When I opened my eyes again, I felt him pull my bra up to my back and finally open the fastener. I took a deep breath and held my breath. He brushed the straps off my shoulders and dropped the little piece of cloth. Sitting in front of him so bared made my insecurity and nervousness reappear.

Seconds later his lips were on mine again as he kissed me slowly, almost as if to calm me down. His hands caressed and kneaded my breasts. I dropped onto my back and slid closer to the head of the bed. Sebastian followed me and covered my entire upper body with little kisses, which almost took my mind. His fingers kept running along the waistband of my black pants.

"Anna," he gasped near my ear, "I want you."

I swallowed, looked into his eyes, which had darkened with need and desire, the pupils dilated.

"Sebastian, I've never ... I am ..." I stammered softly and buried my face in his shoulder. I couldn't quite utter it. I felt the blush rising in my face and my cheeks getting hot .

When I looked up again, his gaze was only disbelief, then he frowned.

"But ... Anna, how old are you?" he asked seriously.

"Don't worry, I'm 23." He seemed relieved, as if a stone had fallen from his heart. His facial features relaxed again.

It had never really bothered me up to this point. And I wanted this deep inside of me Still, I was nervous, also scared.

"But I'm sure. I want you too, so much. I just thought you should know that."

He nodded slowly and kissed me gently, stroking my stomach soothingly. It took away some of my nervousness, but the fear stayed.

Taking my courage together, my hands wandered to his belt and opened it. I struggled briefly with the buttons on his jeans, but shortly afterwards I pushed my pants off his hips. He kicked her off her feet and pushed her off the bed.

Then he was over me again, kissing my neck, sometimes biting lightly or scraping his teeth over it, making me gasp and sigh alternately. I found a hold in his hair, in which my fingers were buried. Under his touching and kissing, I was starting to go insane, almost unable to stand it.

Sebastian's hands wandered down from my shoulders across my sides, brushing the outside of my breasts, then I felt his fingertips on my sides until he finally got there and opened the button on my pants. He pulled himself to his knees and pushed her painfully slowly from my hips, carelessly dropping them to the floor. He was now kneeling by my legs, which I had half raised, and traced with my fingertips from my ankle over my knee to the inside of my thighs. I instinctively spread my legs and my breath quickened. He left his hand motionless on my thigh for a short time, then I felt him put a finger under the hem of my panties and carefully enter me and groaned.

I sat up, leaning on my forearms to watch what he was doing. He looked into my eyes.

"Okay?" He asked harshly. There was a bit of uncertainty in his voice.

"More than that. Sebastian, please. I'm like ... I ... please." I gasped.

"Anna ... you have no idea what you are doing to me, right?"

Suddenly he took my hand and put it on his erection. He was rock hard.

I gasped in surprise, but after the first moment I started to him slowly touching through his tight-fitting shorts. I kept looking him straight in the eye, wanting to see his reaction to my touch. He groaned loudly and cocked his head back.

When I started massaging him firmly through the fabric, he kissed me demanding, taking my breath away. Our tongues fought a passionate struggle, from which no real winner emerged until the end. He took my free hand in his and squeezed it.

After we separated, I took Sebastian's hands and put them on the hem of my panties. Slowly he stroked the fabric, drove lightly over my hill and sighed softly before hooking his fingers into the cuff and slowly taking it off for me.

His eyes were fixed on what he was doing. After he took off the last bit of fabric, I closed my legs out of reflex. He leaned over me, gently brushed my lips with his. He slowly sank down on me, repeating this innocent touch. His hand was on my cheek.

"Please don't hide, you are beautiful," he breathed. His voice was rough and dark and triggered a small wave of excitement in me. I instinctively lifted my pelvis a bit, rubbed his. The friction made him moan , a loud gasp escaped me.

I spread my legs again so that he slid between them and I could feel his erection in the middle, separated only by a layer of fabric. Which only annoyed me increasingly, because the desire gained over my nervousness and I finally wanted to feel Sebastian completely.

So I ran my hands over his back and pushed the shorts off his hips. From the point where I couldn't get any further, he finished my work with a slight grin.

"Right back, little one," he smiled apologetically.

He ran to his suitcase and looked for something in it. His back view was definitely impressive. Nothing but defined muscles and a wonderfully firm butt. When he came back with a silver packet in my hand, I had to swallow hard. For one thing, I was excited by the sight of his naked body, his handsome erection, which rose so steeply from a nest of dark blond hairs that I groaned loudly and bit my lip. On the other hand, a wave of fear came up in me.

My breath quickened when he got back on the bed.

"Hey, are you all right?" He asked with a worried undertone.

"Mh, all right," I replied. I wasn't really sure either.

Sebastian sighed softly and as soon as he was over me he kissed me so breathtakingly tender. When we looked into each other's eyes again, the expression in his calmed me down very much. It gave me security, exuded confidence. My fear subsided. He wouldn't hurt me if he could avoid it. He would be careful.

He leaned back a little and I closed my eyes when I heard him open the package. Groped for him and found his flank on which I stroked up and down. He took my hand and stroked his thumb soothingly over the back of my hand. Then he was over me again, leaning on his forearms so that our hands came to rest next to my head. The other hand went between our bodies and I saw how he embraced himself, positioned himself at my entrance and slowly entered me.

I held my breath, it was just unfamiliar. Very slowly he continued to penetrate me. When he stopped, I moved my hips slightly. Then he kissed me hard, but tenderly and suddenly I felt a sharp pain, closed my eyes tightly, cried out and bit his lip, then heard him groan painfully. When the pain inside me eased a little, I opened my eyes again and stroked his lip with concern.

"Shit, sorry!"

"All right, little one. I'm sorry," he whispered insistently, shaking his head slightly.

With the back of his hand he stroked my temple. Then he kissed me again, infinitely soft. I couldn't taste any blood. But now I felt him slowly entering me, stroking my upper body. It hurt a little less than the first time, but the pain was still enormous. This time he stayed in me, giving me time to get used to the abundance inside me.

"So tight," he mumbled against my lips. He kissed a way to my neck and stroked the outside of my chest with one hand.

When I moved my pelvis a little, he pulled back and I took a deep breath. He slowly built up a rhythm and as the pain gradually subsided, but did not completely disappear, I came closer and closer to his deep impacts.

With every push I felt more and more the excitement that it triggered in me, moved me with him. He was thrusting faster and harder into me and me what that justified. I was sweating slightly, my fingers flew over his body, clawed at his butt. Sebastian groaned. I noticed how I was getting closer to the climax. My mouth no longer obeyed me, I kept making joyful sounds, Sebastian's name the only coherent thing that left my lips.

I felt his fingers at my pleasure point, then everything went under in a whirlpool of vibrant colors.

When I slowly came to, I still felt him thrust deep inside me, but he had slowed the pace. He kept looking at me, a smile on his lips. He pulled himself out of me to the top, only to then slowly push me back in and kissed me lazily.

My hands wrapped around his neck and he gasped as I scratched my nails over the skin there.

As a test, I tensed up my pelvic floor muscles and heard him gasp.

"Beast," he mumbled, but now changed his rhythm. He buried his face on my neck and bit the transition from neck to shoulder, then licked it comfortingly.

His strikes were flatter, faster. He too seemed about to come now. Suddenly he stopped in me and groaned loudly. Then he relaxed and lay still on me. I lazily stroked his sweaty back.

His breathing returned to normal and he raised his head to look at me. I smiled at him, was completely relaxed and happy.

"Come on, let's take a shower and have a nap," he suggests.

"Mh, sounds good."

He pulled his limp limb out of me, which made me feel empty. When I got up from the bed, I felt a bit shaky on my feet.

"Whow," I said.

Sebastian had already gone into the bathroom and I could already hear the shower rustling. When I climbed under the water to him, he pulled me towards him and looked me over.

"What, do I have something on my face?" I asked.

"Apart from your red cheeks and glittering eyes? No," he laughed, "but suits you."

"Idiot," I laughed, slapping him lightly on the Upper arm.

"Hey, aua, don't batter me, they still need me.", He called and rubbed his face, hurt.

"Sissy," I teased, sticking my tongue out at him.

"Very grown up, young lady," he said dryly.

Then he added: "Seriously, are you okay?"

"Everything great. Thank you, Sebastian. My first time was wonderful. "

"Then I'm relieved. I found it very nice with you too. "

He took one of the washcloths and started washing me gently. I did the same afterwards.

I turned off the shower and wrapped myself in one of the fluffy bath towels, then I padded back in room.

I quickly pulled my panties back on and then eyeing critically my blouse. in it, I would not sleep. and sleep naked, I was not used to.

Something helplessly I watched Sebastian, who now also his shorts had dressed again.

"Can. Would you lend me a T-shirt from you? The blouse is not really comfortable and sleep naked ... I usually don't. "I asked quietly.

"Of course no problem."

He handed me a gray, wonderfully soft T-shirt and climbed into bed. He raised the duvet invitingly. I lay down with him and snuggled into his bare chest.

"When do I have to be out of here at the latest?"

"Hm, departure is at 11.30 am. At 6 am at the latest . Sorry. But wake me up before you go, yes?"

"Alright." It wasn't really that real. A bitter aftertaste, which I hadn't expected, remained.

"Anna, can I ask you something?"

"Wasn?

"Why ... being a virgin at 23 is ... unusual ..."

"Didn't turn out. Why, when was your first time?" I avoided.

"There I was 17. With my girlfriend at the time. Was a ... expandable experience. Neither of us really had a plan for what we were doing, "he says, laughing." The times after that it got better. Practice makes perfect. "

"Yes, Master." I laughed.

He didn't ask any more and left it at that.

I got up again to set my alarm clock to 5.30 and felt a twitch in my abdomen. I grimaced in pain.

Then I snuggled back into bed with Sebastian.

"Good night," I said,

"Sleep well," he replied, placing a kiss on the back of my neck.

Just minutes later, my alarm clock rang. Sebastian wrapped his arm around my stomach. I carefully loosen it and get up as quietly as possible. I suppressed a sound of pain. The tugging in the abdomen hurt more than a few hours ago.

I took my clothes, scurried into the bathroom, got dressed and tried to adjust my appearance to some extent. I quickly tied a ponytail and distributed some tinted day cream that I always had in my handbag. Had to be enough.

I stood undecided in the bathroom door, wondering whether I should really wake him up or just go. However, I didn't have the heart - stupid, sentimental, soft heart - and woke him up.

"Good morning," he mumbled sleepily. I looked at him.

"Hey. I just wanted to say ... I'll go now. I found the night with you really beautiful. Thanks again. "I kissed him one last time.

Then I put the borrowed sleep shirt on the bed and turned to go.

" Hey, wait, will you give me your number? I ... would like to contact you again. "

"Sure," I said flatly and wrote it on a piece of paper.

"Thank you Anna. And ... here." He held out the gray shirt to me. "Keep it. Give me back when the opportunity arises. ", He winked.

I just nodded and left the room.

I quickly disappeared into one of the staff corridors and made sure that I came out of the hotel before anyone else saw me. When I came out of the supplier's entrance,

I never heard from him again.

The End.

Summer in Austin

I experienced the following story in exactly the same way during my first vacation in the USA. It had a lasting impact on me and my relationship with experienced women. Some details that were not essential for the course of the action have been changed. Otherwise, this was a very drastic and extremely awesome experience for me.

Finally done!!! I passed my pre-diploma with flying colors and thanks to my lucky knack for speculating on a number of stocks, I was able to fulfill two wishes: on the one hand I was able to concentrate on my studies for the next 3 semesters without financial worries, and on the other hand I was able to enjoy a long-cherished vacation dream fulfill: A trip of several weeks to the USA - especially to Texas and Colorado - to see the country and its people and above all to hear a lot of country and southern music live.

After my arrival in Dallas and the obligatory sightseeing tour (6th Floor Museum, Reunion Tower and various art galleries), I (Robert, student, mid 20s with a sporty figure) made myself on the way to Austin, the music capital of Texas and one of the cities, after 2 days best places for live music ever.

A motel near the University of Texas campus was quickly found, a refreshing shower taken, and I was ready for nightlife. I didn't really feel like driving a car. Experience has taught me that music, nightlife and sober rarely go together. Then with the shuttle bus to the State Capitol of Texas and straight onto Sixth Street, the musical center of Austin. It was awesome. Club after club followed here and without exception live music of any kind: jazz, rock country, everything was represented and I was right in the middle of it without a plan as to what would be the best decision.

The clubs weren't crowded early in the evening, so I decided to go to a bar where a band was covering a number of songs from the Atlanta Rhythm Section - and it was pretty good. As it turns out, the best decision during the entire vacation should be.

The place was a classic music bar with various bars throughout the room and a few reserved tables in front of the dance floor. The gallery consisted practically of a single elongated bar with a great view of the entire restaurant and - how could it be otherwise - was unfortunately already fully occupied. Then we searched for a place at a somewhat remote bar and finally ordered a fresh beer.

The restaurant was increasingly filled with a diverse audience: students, couples, older couples, men and women on the hunt for an adventure - everything was represented. In short: I had a lot of fun, danced a couple of times with some women without any result and had a great chat with my changing neighbors at the bar. The band played excellently and I had a good overview of everything. Of course, I paid particular attention to the female guests, but somehow to no avail. Either the ladies were accompanied by men or just not interesting for me.

Over the course of the evening I noticed a lady at the other end of the bar who seemed to me to be more than a tad too young for her age. I estimated she was in her early 50s (which turned out to be completely wrong), a very athletic figure with shoulder-length brunette hair. The skirt was significantly shorter than it seemed appropriate for her age, but the blouse was all the more scarce, so that the top buttons threatened to burst at any moment and just looking at the high heels my ankle almost automatically twisted. The appearance was extremely sexy and also caused a certain tightness in my pants without that touching me. Don't stop my prey scheme !!

She was immediately the focus of all the men at the bar, danced from time to time and successfully fended off the all too often uncouth attempts at advances with a certain charm. I had fun watching what was going on and couldn't help but feel a little bit jarring when a man tried again just to find out that he really didn't have a chance.

It went on for a while and I was on the dance floor again. When I came back I was surprised. The lady had sat down in the free space next to me, smiled at me and said only: "So if you don't come to me, don't ask me to dance and just watch as old men clumsily clumsy me, then I'll sit next to you. Maybe we'll start talking. By the way, I'm Deborah, but you can call me Debbie ". I didn't expect that now. But somehow I was also a little proud, at least the looks of the surrounding men suggested a certain envy factor.

I introduced myself briefly and explained to Debbie that she had to apologize for my sometimes strange English, since I am only a tourist and therefore sometimes have to practice a little on the vocabulary. In any case, the first ice was broken and she moved a little closer to me. We had a lot of fun, danced together several times, had a few drinks and simply enjoyed the evening. It was finally Friday. At some point after a dance round she put her arm around me and said succinctly "It is just more fun to dance with a young man and to enjoy the evening, who knows how to treat a lady than with a rough buffalo who asks for a drink after a drink and still wonders if he gets a rejection ". Her short something slipped,

Obviously, I had enjoyed this look for too long and probably had looked a little too closely. In any case, she came very close to me and whispered in my ear: "Do you like what you see" and with a look at my slightly dented pants she said "The answer is obvious. I also like your answer by the way".

I was never particularly interested in experienced women, especially when the age difference was so large (Debbie was 68, I was 25). But her much younger appearance, her style and her appearance made me really excited. Anyway, my cock ached considerably because of the tightness in my pants. Before I could say anything, Debbie said "I think it's time for us to go" and with a look at the bulge in my pants and especially quietly so that the others around could not hear it. "But only when you can walk properly again. I want to take care of him a little bit after all."

The question about me or about you was answered relatively quickly. Debbie had an apartment just outside and hadn't come by car either so she could enjoy the evening accordingly. A taxi was found quickly and we were there 10 to 15 minutes later.

The word apartment was an understatement for her apartment. It was a 3 room apartment with loft character in a very modern apartment complex quite high up, which was simply huge. Very modern and very tastefully decorated. The whole thing was cut so that on the courtyard side there was still a covered terrace, which was probably more than twice the size of my own apartment. On the terrace were very modern and comfortable lounge furniture and a whirlpool, which had enough space for 6 or 8 people.

Debbie must have been able to read my mind. "Even if you can't take a look here, the neighbors can hear us and they WILL hear us. I'll go freshen up a bit and you can set up a glass of champagne for us. The champagne is in the fridge and you can find the glasses in the kitchen." Spoke and disappeared.

I took care of the drinks, sat on the couch standing in the middle of the room and slowly I began to have doubts about what I'm doing here. Sure, I was on vacation and also single, but a woman who was only 1 year younger than my grandmother - the very thought of it frightened me and made my blood flow back into my brain. Somehow I had to get out of the situation safely without losing my face.

Just as I was collecting my thoughts, Debbie came back. She had obviously showered and changed a little. Breathtaking. She had on a black leather skirt with side zippers, which could only be called a belt and with which she could not bend down, she had exchanged her blouse for a black leather coursage that was cut so low that her nipples protruded almost completely and instead She ran towards me with high heels with black over the knee boots that just looked awesome. No grandmother looked like that.

"I hope you like my new outfit, I didn't want to go out dressed like that, but that's just right for a cozy evening at home." We toasted ourselves with champagne and she sat next to me, whispered in my ear "Relax and don't think about anything. We have the whole night and if you want the whole weekend." Slowly she started to open my shirt and caress my skin with her hands, not demanding but very carefully and very slowly. I was alternately hot and cold. My thoughts about how I could get out of this situation were completely gone. This woman was nibbling on me according to all the rules of art and I couldn't get enough of it.

My shirt was completely off and Debbie was slowly starting to spoil my nipples with her fingers and tongue. It was like 100 lightning strikes me. I had never experienced anything like this, although I was not exactly inexperienced in this area. She leaned slightly over me so that her nipples touched my chest and opened my pants to free my cock from his prison.

My lust knew hardly any limits and she started to jerk my cock and massage my balls. I took hold of her thighs and carefully felt my way up her venus mound. As my hand slowly but surely slid up, her groans grew louder, more demanding and violent. Debbie wasn't wet, she was wet like a waterfall. Her pubic hair dripped with lust. I slowly worked my way to your pleasure grotto and started massaging her labia. She groaned and when I started to finger her, her muscles twitched and she let her lust run free.

In the meantime I had got rid of my pants and let Debbie allow my cock. She only jerked me for a short time, just so that I didn't come, which drove me crazy. I had never had sex so exciting. She sat on the couch in front of me and began to spoil my cock with her tongue. The tip of her tongue only touched my glans briefly and she stopped when I started to sink my cock in her mouth. She challenged me, turned me on - only to NOT let me come at the crucial moment. That could not go well in the long run. Debbie looked at me with a smile until I couldn't. I pushed her head very carefully forward and started to push my cock deeper into her mouth. She blew my cock with an intensity that I had never seen before. It literally sucked me out and it didn't take long for me to explode completely. I pumped thrust by thrust into her throat until I couldn't and she never let out a drop. The sperm dripped from the corners of her mouth and we kissed uncontrollably until we were both pretty exhausted on the sofa.

"I hope you still have a little bit of it left. I'm far from finished with you," she whispered in my ear. "Let's take the champagne into the bedroom and then you want to feel deep inside me. You should impale me until I just scream. I want to feel it when you come in me".

A few moments later we had arrived in the bedroom, which was very spartan but also very tastefully decorated. The double bed was huge and littered with tons of pillows. Debbie lit a series of scented candles that emitted a pleasant scent and intensified the erotic tension that was already there.

I was desperately looking for a place to drop the champagne because the bedside tables were filled with scented candles, Debbie's jewelry and some very nice wristwatches. "Put the jewelry and the watches in a drawer and don't let yourself be distracted. Better come to me and take care of me." She looked at me with a cheeky and seductive smile and began to unbutton her coursage. My cock was extremely pleased with this performance and I helped Debbie get rid of the rest of her clothes. Her breasts were firm and taut and her nipples were quite steep. "Do you like my tits?" And without waiting for my answer, she said "What cosmetic corrections can do .....".

In any case, I sucked her nipples like a newborn on the mother's breast and her reaction to it showed me that she enjoyed it. I started to bite very lightly and carefully and to gently spoil her breasts with my teeth. She was just as ready as I was, and her moans grew louder and more demanding. I slowly moved my tongue down, circled her belly button, poured a little champagne over her stomach and started licking the champagne off my skin. It literally exploded under this treatment. Now I could pay her back: I read for a very long time until I buried my tongue in her wet column. The cunt juice ran down between her thighs and she fired at me "Lick me .... Deeper .... Let me come ...... Yes, don't stop, please don't stop ....."

In the meantime my cock was really wet and I was ready to take Debbie. I sat in front of her and started to lightly touch her entrance with my cock. Her moans were automatically loud and her tone was cool, almost obscene, without appearing ordinary. "Give me your cock ..... Fuck me properly ..... Show me that you are a great stallion." She massaged my back with her hands and tried to push me forward. She wanted to be fucked - right now.

I moved forward and carefully entered her. Her cunt was still amazingly tight and well lubricated, so it was no problem for me to sink my cock deep into it. She crossed her legs behind me and our fucking speed was found straight away. I pushed deep into her and she started to wriggle under me. With every push she pushed my cock deeper into her pelvis with her legs. Our rhythm gradually increased and I started to push harder and deeper. She groaned and screamed her lust out of herself and obviously couldn't get enough. "Push me .... impale me ... spray me full ... wet my cunt ...."

This bitch didn't let me rest. I pushed her as deep and hard as I could - and she cheered me on pretty dirty and still wanted more. I noticed that she was about to come, but wasn't ready yet. The rhythm became faster, the moaning louder and the movements of our bodies more and more violent. After a while I noticed how her body stiffened and her vaginal muscles contracted. With a primal scream that Joe Cocker would have honored her orgasm unloaded. "Jaaaaaaaaaaaaaaaa ..... I'm comingeeeee". She screamed and gasped as if there was no tomorrow. I slowed down to let Debbie enjoy that feeling and give her a break.

Slowly the juice was noticeable in my eggs and I noticed that I was soon ready. I was still deep in Debbie's cunt and almost completely pulled my cock out with every push, only to penetrate it even harder afterwards. My hands worked on her nipples and breasts. My eggs were boiling and I knew I couldn't hold it for long. Her pelvic movements only increased my lust and I literally pinned her with my cock. It was not long before I unloaded myself into her cunt with a series of huge spurts that were correspondingly loudly accompanied. The sweat dripped from my forehead and I was pretty exhausted. This woman had killed me. But I was quite satisfied in the truest sense of the word.

It was quite early and both of us were pretty exhausted by this great night, so that we both fell asleep pretty tired but incredibly relaxed shortly afterwards. I spent the weekend with Debbie and we fucked our hearts out. She had to go to her sons in California on Monday and wanted to do a few things there for a few days, but said "If you are still there next weekend, I would be very happy to do it again".

Of course I was still there and the repetition turned into 2 weeks, in which we also did a lot. Debbie showed me some of the nicest corners in and around Austin. Too often we were mistaken for mother and daughter, which often led to some irritation, but somehow we didn't care. We had sex at least 2 to 3 times a day without it ever getting boring (yes and also on the terrace, but that during the day). When I moved on to Colorado on my vacation, we were both very happy to have had such a great and great time together.

After this vacation, I no longer had a younger partner, although the age difference was also limited. All partners were about 10 to 15 years older than me and I have not regretted this decision. Not until today!

Addendum

Years after my vacation in the USA, I still maintained a penpal friendship with Debbie that was of a serious nature, although there were also some odd letters. In the meantime, she lived in Amarillo and invited me to celebrate her 75th birthday. Due to a change of job and a longer break associated with it, I was also able to accept this invitation. She really wanted to pick me up from the airport. She still looked gorgeous and had obviously given herself various cosmetic touch-ups that definitely did not fail to work. We had a lot to talk about on the way to your property, which was just outside. The most important thing for her was that our meeting should not necessarily go around in the family circle, because on the occasion of this birthday her whole family was there and they certainly would not have understood that. But that went without saying. We agreed that I would have met Debbie on one of her trips abroad.

It was a little weird to talk to her two sons, both of whom were about 15 years older than me, knowing that their mother and I screwed our hearts out for two weeks. I was grinning a little when Richard and Matthew said goodbye to their mother and Richard said that his mother should welcome me with exactly the same hospitality that she experienced from me - which she did after all the celebrations - but certainly different than he expected.

We still had contact for several years, which then suddenly and suddenly broke off. She was also no longer available by phone. In 2003 I received a package with a watch and a multi-page letter from Matthew from California. It turned out that this was one of the watches that Debbie's box was on. He informed me that his mother died in a riding accident shortly before her 80th birthday. The horse shied away and threw off its mother. In doing so, she was thrown against a boulder and was immediately dead.

In the course of working through the entire estate, they came across the diaries of their mother, in which she had written down one or the other Tete a Tete with significantly younger men - including me, of course. The family was more than shocked by this way of life, especially because they had written down all the details of my stay on the occasion of their birthday. That was probably a little too much for you. After a whole number of years in the country and it was his mother's will that I should get this watch, he obviously wanted to clean up and fulfill this last will, albeit very late. I don't think he and his brother really understood what happened between me and Debbie.

The End.

The PC course

Recently I attended a basic course for a PC operating system. Since the operating system is still somewhat exotic (Ubuntu), the participants could be counted on one hand. So we only used one row of tables in the classroom.

The subject matter was interesting, the participants and the course leader Peter motivated. However, Peter was still new to the industry and therefore one day he was visited or checked by his trainer in the course. Anita Meier was actually an unobtrusive but confident woman. I estimate her age at around 45 years. She had a good figure and was wearing a simple dress.

There was enough free space in the second row, so she sat down on a chair behind my neighbor. We then started the repetitions as always. Peter gave us a small task which we had to solve in 10 minutes. Until then, the course required my full attention. But I quickly solved the task. I turned to get a sheet from the printer. I immediately noticed two bare feet under the table behind me. Red-painted nails captivated my eyes. They seemed to play with each other quite innocently. A quick look at the owner of these feet showed me that she was immersed in her documents.

Having my papers, I returned to my place of work. Distracted by a problem from my neighbor, I almost tripped over her feet. I just brushed it. She immediately pulled her back and we exchanged a quick look. This puzzled me because I could not interpret it correctly. It wasn't actually a smile, but it wasn't just friendly. However, I was too captivated by the evaluation of my work to take a closer look at this view.

Then when the instructor joined my neighbor to solve his problem, I turned to them. Again I noticed movement in the corner of my eye. It was her bare feet again.

I'm really not a foot fetishist, so she took a closer look at me.

They were well cared for, as far as I could not judge this, or not recently pedicured professionally, because the painted nails had color damage and I saw a little cornea on the big toe. As mentioned; I didn't really like feet in general. So my eye kept walking along my legs. They were beautifully slim but of course no longer youthfully tender. But the pleasure ended at the knees. The table top blocked my view. Apparently she was still captivated by her documents. This showed me a control look.

Next to me, Peter and Hermann were still busy with their problem and ignored me. So I was able to tie my shoes in peace. This, of course, more to observe the special circumstances than that it was really necessary.

What I saw then exceeded my expectations. I already "knew" her lower legs. They were shaved or depilated in some other way. Rather pale, which is not surprising since spring was still young, and slightly marked by their age (or rather: their life experience?). So my eye brushed quickly over her shins, got over my knees and set off on new shores.

This bank (in the form of your dress) was surprisingly far away. I saw a shapely thigh, because the hem of her dress was about the edge of the chair. "Is her dress really that short?" I thought. "I would have noticed that when she entered the room." Or was it just covered by the monitors?

I almost flinched when she moved. I was completely lost in these thoughts.

She crossed her legs. This allowed me to take a closer look at her thighs. There might have been a few grams too much, but certainly not many.

Hardly have you been lucky enough to get an erotic kick unexpectedly, because I have to admit that my heart rate increased a bit due to this special situation, and thoughts came up that could have worked even better: "If she had carried out this movement with the other leg, she would have I might even catch a glimpse of her panties. "

Well, I'm married. However, my wife's sexual activities are kept to a minimum. She didn't refuse sex, but she behaved extremely passively and that tends to turn her off. That's why I started feeling more and more underutilized.

More and more I satisfied myself with the thought of accidental insights into decolletes, enjoyable viewing of well-shaped rear views or trousers of the ladies' world that were almost painfully cramped at the crotch. Everything reveals itself freely and free of charge in bus and train. "After all, these are convincing advantages of public transport and sometimes make reading a newspaper superfluous," I would tell everyone. It is good to have one, however, because clothing does not always hide the treacherous consequences of such studies this sight of course to the higher-class trophies, which was not without consequences, but thanks to the stooped posture and the subsequent sitting this should not be a problem,

but now it was time to show up again.

My eyes were still on her legs, then wandered off to the course participants and returned to Anita at normal height (I secretly decided to call her by her first name when I was so close to her). Actually I just wanted to turn forward when I was startled. Something was wrong here. But what was it that only bothered me? Instinctively (or drive-controlled?) My eyes were on her chest. This was not lavish but of a pleasant dimension. I simply took note of the high neckline and the decorative necklace.

Now it dawned on me. During my inspections, I got used to looking for signs of the position and size of the nipples. But there was nothing to look for. She had put on a jacket, so it seemed cool. This was also not uncommon in an air-conditioned room. Together with the removed shoes and the very high hem compared to the non-existent decollete, there was a discrepancy that gave me a few seconds to think.

How it could not have been otherwise: I suddenly noticed that she was looking at me. Of course, she knew where my eyes came from (where I was staring at before? - I don't know). Although I'm not macho and should rather feel caught, I held her gaze. Surprisingly, this also without turning red (presumably too much blood was used in my tail). That strange look in her eyes again. For a moment I was captivated by him. I interrupt him briefly to catch her breasts again and restore him to challenge her. I succeeded in doing this, but then I had to smile away from her with a smile.

Just in time, because the actual class seemed to start and required my concentration. Better: would have required my concentration. With bloodlessness in the head and Anita's gaze in the memory, one could not think of keeping up. So I had to do something. But what?

"Go out for a minute and get some fresh air? I thought. "My trousers are tightening something. I wouldn't be embarrassed if they saw it." It shot through my head. "But Peter, would he see it? And the colleagues? "Now it was getting hot and still gave me a shiver. Really uncomfortable. I decided to stay and look for a candy in my briefcase. This distracted me and I was able to attend classes again.

A short time later, Anita intervened with an interim question. Maybe to test whether he would find the thread on it again? In any case, the participants were also involved in this conversation.

I turned around so I could look her in the eye as I made my comment. In the end, my eyes accidentally fell under the table.

It was already back to normalizing my body functions. Before that, she was sitting at the table. I was able to see her right leg a little from the side, as she was sitting at one of my workplaces. But now both legs were pointing in my direction. They were not folded over each other as before, but stood next to each other and were certainly 20 cm apart. This did not change when she continued the conversation with Peter. She even moved her knees slightly up and down.

"Is she doing this on purpose? What should I do? ", I thought. It was tight again in my pants. There was nothing to be seen above her knees because of the table. I didn't want to tie my shoes again.

" Come on, come up with something! " I urged myself on.

The briefcase was on the wrong side. Ah, office chair, elevator. So slowly let air out and sink. Yes that brings something. But what is that? Only 10 cm more to see. So adjust the backrest. Another 5 cm. So I wasn't mistaken earlier, she had really handsome legs. How further?

"Now done, pull yourself together!" I said to myself.

Just in time. As soon as I looked Anita in the face again, she turned back to me. Fortunately not with a question, because I hadn't heard anything from the conversation. " Just "with that strange look that I couldn't classify.

"Damn, what kind of situation is that," I thought. I just had to tear myself away from her.

I also succeeded physically. I apparently looked at the material and clicked on the speaker's actions on the screen. I was only mentally concerned with working out a strategy so that I could take a look under her skirt.

Mechanically I switched to bash, entered commands that I didn't understand and started a program that should have some quirks.

Again there is a problem with Hermann. The control unit with which you bring the screen of the course participants on the projector seems (fortunately) not to work. Peter sets off again, stands between me and Herrmann, compares screens and command memory and searches for the error.

I saw an opportunity. Anita's head was now covered by a monitor.

"So go, go diving station too.", I thought to myself. Thinking and acting take place simultaneously in such an emergency anyway.

Of course, the pulse is also up, so the body is still capable of top performance (thanks to regular fitness training).

But now I am seized with horror: shoes on my feet and skirt hem on

my knees! "What's going on?" I pondered. "Why this change?"

I sit down in shock. Obviously a little too suddenly, because Peter turned to me as if he wanted to check whether I still had all the cups in the cupboard.

Anita looked at me too. I was confused now, but saw a clearly apologetic look. She even pointed to Peter with her eyes. So that seemed to be the reason for the change in their behavior. All I could do was raise my eyebrows questioningly and I turned back to the front.

The situation was now serious.

So it was clearly their intention to treat me to this pleasure or to make me hot. Peter was somehow between us. But how and why? I clearly felt her eyes on my back. Participation in class was definitely out of the question.

I clearly needed a break, fresh air, coffee or another distraction and decided to sign up for a toilet break. Almost at the same time, Peter said that the long break would be preferred so that he could discuss with Mrs. Meier. That came naturally to me. Due to the excitement, everything in my pants had calmed down again so that I could stroll safely into the break room.

When I got there I got a drink and stood at the window. On the one hand to organize my thoughts, on the other hand to signal to the others that I was not after the usual discussions about tricks and tricks.

It also worked very well. I came to the conclusion that this was clearly a unique opportunity. I had to act.

It was positive that Anita had to pass the break room if she was to leave us.

The negative was that I had no idea how to address them.

Time was short but an idea was not within reach. And I already heard heels in the corridor. Well, that could have been another woman.

Bad luck, because I hear her say goodbye to the other participants. That couldn't and shouldn't be true.

"That certainly doesn't apply to me!" I decided.

I had to act. I immediately turned and followed her. I caught up with her one floor below.

"Anita!" I heard myself calling.

She stopped abruptly and turned to me. As a result, we had already fallen below the usual decency distance. "Yes, Georg," she replied. Obviously she picked up my name or looked it up from the list. It was actually common for us to take a course in the computer environment. However, she did not know us and had spoken to you Barrier fell between us.

Obviously she didn't expect to talk to me, neither did I want to have one. We just faced each other and looked at each other. You again with their strange look and I possibly (probably) greedily because I clearly only wanted one more thing: touching, feeling, being close to her.

"How much can I risk?" I thought.

Without saying a word I put my hands on her upper arms and gently pulled them towards me without losing eye contact. I felt no significant resistance and our kiss was only a logical continuation of it.

I don't know what she felt. I only felt my desire and registered her consent. It behaved passively but was clearly willing. So I started to insert the tongue, penetrated between her lips without resistance, bumped into her teeth, passed it and found the tongue. This immediately began to communicate with mine and they quickly agreed on the fighting style and intensity.

Now she had her arms wrapped around me too, so there was no reason to hesitate. Nevertheless, we had to pause out of breath. Not our eyes. They made almost the same contortions as before the tongues.

"Where?", I couldn't get any more.

Because we couldn't stay here in the corridor. I wanted more. She just shrugged her shoulders. Actually, she had to know her way better than I did, or she thought in other dimensions or her courage left her.

"Attack is the best defense," I thought to myself.

At least I wanted a second kiss. I almost challenged him. I wasn't sure if she hesitated, but felt how she pressed against me.

This was not without consequences. Feeling her breasts, approaching the last few centimeters and letting my hand wander into her cross to tie her down to me were one.

If she had still had any doubts about my intentions, they should be cleared up now. No resistance felt now either.

"What am I doing?" Goes through my head. But I'm not looking for a solution, I'm only now becoming aware of how far I've gone.

"An affair has never been considered before, only the quiet enjoyment" . I heard my conscience.

There was no time for that now. I heard voices and footsteps.

"Come with me!" I whispered to her.

She actually nodded. I took her in my arms and led her down the stairs. We crossed a crowd. I simply led them down in the hope of finding a basement which is also one and not an expanded basement. Just like when I was a teenager.

The gods are actually on my side. The stairs end very old-fashioned in the basement. The same gear as above.

"Not ideal," I think, and drag her under the stairs.

Thanks to the old construction, the headroom is relatively far back and it is a little dim because there is little light coming down from the ground floor.

So far she has not made a sound, which should surprise me because of her appearance. But I didn't have time to think about it.

"She was willing to be brought here, so she is also ready for more," I thought to myself. So I turned her back to the wall, took the bag that she had hung over her shoulder and placed it next to us the floor.

That look again.

Not the right time to think about it: "I want to feel you."

We sink into a kiss. I forget everything else. But don't forget what I want. My hands go on a journey of discovery, explore the flanks up to the armpits. She puts her hands around my neck, pulls me close and intensifies the kiss.

"That is a clear sign," the strategist in me informs me.

So the next thing I want to do is explore her breast. Take a little air between us and put your hands forward. Yes, that feels good.

She got too little air, interrupted the kiss and rested on my cheek. Kissing her ear drove me on. I drove down the sides, whereupon she took a deep breath and I turned.

"I don't want to go to the Blessed Sacrament so quickly," I want her prefer to say.

Just one step closer for more feeling. Nevertheless, I felt that I had to increase the pressure a bit to confirm my long-term intentions. I clearly felt the ribs through the clothes. When I reached the bottom, on the one hand I felt the end of the knitted jacket and on the other hand a slight tremor. So I changed the direction of my research again. With a layer less between us, I slid up rib by rib again.

I soon got to the bottom bra of her bra, ignoring this border encompassing both breasts and kneading them lightly. Despite the two remaining layers of fabric (one of which could be quite thin, but I didn't know that yet), I felt a hardening in the middle. So your buds responded too. This confirmed my impressions and encouraged me to continue.

But I want to look at them, because even if I make it clear what I want, I don't want to force them to do anything, but I do persuade them. She still had that indefinable, I thought, now dreamy look. Again I kneaded my two conquests a little more. She shivered again slightly, but clearly enjoyed it. So there was no going back.

The goal could only be: less material between us.

So put your hand back down to eliminate the next layer.

However, it turned out that I had not probed the conditions too closely or that the concentration was somewhere else. She was wearing a one-piece dress! Now I didn't want to be under my skirt. The risk was too great for me after the previous reaction.

It was still too early for "everything or nothing". So there was only the detour via the back.

With the left hand still kneading her breast, the right hand sought the way via the waist and cross in the back. It was so exciting to touch another woman again, that I always had to brake a little, because I still didn't have the impression that Anita often nibbled on strange men because of lust, but wanted to be conquered step by step.

"Keep your hands where they are," I tell myself. "She's still enjoying it, and so am I."

I was missing her lips and tongue again. So get into the fight. Here we clearly had the same wavelength and almost ate each other up.

As beautiful as that was, it couldn't be all.

"I want to feel more of you," I said to her only in thought and pressed my lower body lightly against hers.

She was irritated that I noticed from her kisses.

"You convince," says the devil in me.

I obeyed and pressed myself against her even more.

The leeway to the wall was long gone. My right hand would have reported that too, but it was simply ignored.

All feelings were focused on my pelvic area. I clearly felt her pubic bone on my cock. However, he suffered in the meantime because he could not take the place due to him.

"There is a need for action here," I thought, hoping that she would not misunderstand this. But it had to be.

"At worst, you have an unbeatable memory of jerking off tonight," I think, taking the left one from my chest and slowly lowering it notice how she stiffened. I wanted to stroke her back reassuringly, but realized that it was not possible.

"No way I will lose contact.", So I pressed it with his right hand in the back more me, and set the left my cock. Not without the kiss almost get really obligatory upright.

At the retreat of the left drive I actually didn't intentionally with the back of my hand over her abdomen. Immediately he started to shake and her kiss became even more stormy.

"It can't be that wrong," I thought and stayed where I was, but rubbed my cock more against her pubic area. Now she moaned in my mouth too. Oh, that was a great feeling. She is now really clinging to me. Obviously, she was very close to her first orgasm.

My wife was not that fast in her prime, although I thought I knew all the secret places.

The devil rode me well because I stopped my movements, just held them and pressed them to me. Again she broke the kiss, but this time she wasn't looking for me, but looked at me with a look that would have triumphed if I hadn't just been horny. He was expressing supplication. Actually not only this: supplication and what? What was it that I couldn't see?

"No matter. That can not be to my disadvantage if I continue now "went through my head.

So entranced and proud of this situation I continued. I moved my pelvis, the back of my hand and pressed it with my right hand again. Your reaction annoyed me so much that I almost jerked off, but I didn't want to.

"Why am I suddenly so scalded?" I thought, probably preventing my effusion.

For Anita, on the other hand, there was no turning back. She started to moan so strongly that I had to close her mouth with a kiss, we didn't want to hear and maybe be discovered.

as quickly as it started, it was back to the end. compared to before, I needed but both arms to hold her. her head rested on my shoulder and they obviously needed a break.

Amazing for me was the The fact that despite this incomparable situation, I started to analyze the situation.

"The only unknown in this system is her look," I concluded. "If you know what that means, then it's yours," I said to myself a little arrogantly. "That's exactly it: not arrogant, but dominant she had to feel me. "That was how I had acted. But since this was not in my nature, I did not recognize the look she replied: submissive.

I had to control that. How could it? Certainly her look would now simply be grateful I just wanted to try it out proudly but unsatisfied as I was.

"What do I want to do now?" I asked myself. "Skin," was the answer. "I just want to feel it directly."

So I decided to go "whole".

By moving my whole body, I made her understand that it was going on now.

"I want to feel you now. Turn around! "I whispered into her ear in a moderate command tone.

A bit astonished, but with exactly the look of her eyes, she looked at me. But of course she turned without saying a word. I took her arms and put my hands on the wall with my palms at head level. "Hopefully she realizes that the hands should stay there too." I still thought and leaned my lower body against her butt so that she could still feel my cock, which was still full, of course. And already she put her head with her left ear on her hands so that I could see her in profile. It was not inconvenient for me because at least I could roughly assess her feelings.

Still I could hardly believe it. Two hours ago I was only looking forward to the interesting material and now I was in the middle of the best adventure in years.

In my euphoria, however, I could only allow such thoughts for a tenth of a second and I could not stop. My hands automatically lay on her waist, hiked up and down under the jacket, so that my fingertips should still be able to enjoy the base of my chest. But a few centimeters further her arms pressed against my body blocked my way.

"Attention, she's getting tense," I concluded. "It can't stay that way! Make it clear to her again where to go and then relax." When I pressed my fingers into the non-existent space, the pressure decreased only slightly. A turn of my hands was enough as a sign of my intention, the arms went a little away from the body.

So start over. Hands to the side and thumbs to the back. With my eyes closed, I enjoyed this way a few times over the waist to the hip and back again under the armpits. "That should almost feel like a massage," I thought, and after a few such movements I heard a slight sigh.

However, I did not want to lose sight of my goal and shifted my job more to my back. The thumbs were now next to the spine and so my palm and fingers stroked or massaged her back. As expected, the next stage goal was on the spine: the zipper. So this time all the way up over the shoulder blades to the neck to explore the end of the fabric. A small detour to the neck and shoulder was not only used to camouflage this observation. It was just a good feeling to feel her skin. So far I have acted with my eyes closed and absorbed the shape and grip of this wonderful body.

Before and for the next step, however, I wanted to see her face so that I could adapt my actions to her behavior.

She still had her eyes closed. As far as I could tell, her facial features were relaxed. Logical that I felt the zipper and slowly opened it. No reaction.

"So she expected me to continue like this," I tell myself. "Hopefully her limits are still far away."

I only noticed how long such a fastener can be when I hit my waistband. In no way did I want to lose the contact of my cock with her butt. He was just starting to dig into her buttocks so nicely.

Losing no time, my fingers plunged into the newly opened terrain and precisely reached the boundary between pleasantly soft, warm skin and the delicate fabric of her underwear.

"What is she wearing?" I wondered. "It doesn't seem to be profane cotton."

She seemed to know exactly what I was thinking and feel a faint smile played around her lips. "So the short massage did what it should. The trust is there. "

Her eyes were closed and she waited. My second hand also started to travel under the dress. She pushed it apart and stroked the conquered skin, got a run-up on her neck and slid purposefully in the valley between them Shoulder blades down to the bra. Once there, the situation was first explored.

"Aha. Not the very narrow bands. He also has two nice portions to hold," I muse. "What do I do only when the fastener is in the front?"

Fortunately, the subsequent inspection found that this concern was unfounded.

"It is incredibly exciting to just feel it and make a picture of what it looks like," I agree with myself, because my view was blocked by a layer of wool.

I was actually not a friend of many words, so it amazed me even that in such a situation I still had the time and desire to talk to myself, at least this made me think that maybe I should not only think about myself but also about Anita.

"I would like to whisper tenderly in her ear, how good she feels, how it excites me, how she excites and excites me.", But after I had to order her to turn and pull her arms apart, it wouldn't be what should I do?

"Do what you do best and want anyway," I thought. "Stroking, massaging, researching." But

first I wanted to do research. The material and the content of the bra came in handy for such studies.

The soft and smooth material of the back and side part merged into something rougher in the cups.

"This is certainly such a semi-transparent lace," my thoughts stimulated me even more. I knew from a (secret) look at laundry catalogs that beautiful packaging strengthens the desire for the content. I always imagined how this material should also be exciting to wear.

This also came true, because the buds seemed to be a little harder than before. A good sign. So back, feel the closure, open it, let it slide gently and immediately back towards the buds. This time, however, I only felt delicate skin. The breasts still had to be freed from the cups. It could be a sign of the time (of their age) or even the attitude that this was not so easy. But firstly, this was a mature woman and secondly, I didn't lack the experience, but a little more up-to-date training for such activities. And I've wanted this for a long time.

It was just wonderful to hold her like that. The more skin I conquered, the more my arousal increased. I noticed this from the fact that I almost pressed Anita against the wall. The back of my hands came into contact with the wall and her pelvis could no longer avoid my pushing.

I just wanted to get closer and closer to her. Kissing her neck, ear and cheek, I did the same. As far as she could turn her head she came to meet me immediately, so that we sank into a never-ending kiss.

Only now did I realize that her dress was also under a lot of tension. By pushing it apart with both arms, I wanted it to slide up, but couldn't because of my pressure. As a result, it should pull on the shoulders. So I had to break the contact with her beautiful butt for better or worse. I also had to interrupt the kiss because this time I lacked breath, I was hot, I was hot for more and hopefully she was too.

It didn't seem that bad at all because I moved my arms a little to the side when I saw the dress slide up. But now I also realized that part of my tension was due to my tight pants.

I had to change this because my tail bumped into the waistband of my pants or underpants. Without thinking I took a hand from her chest and wanted to straighten my cock. But somehow that was not possible. So I freed him for simplicity.

Button open, zipper down and the elastic band of the underpants under the scrotum are movements practiced a thousand times during urination. They are usually carried out with two hands, but it can also be done quickly and efficiently with one hand.

That was probably too fast for Anita too. Probably not so much the action in and of itself, but rather the knowledge of the apparent purpose.

Moving her hips brought me back to reality. She wanted to turn away, looked at me in alarm, and wanted to say something.

"Now you screwed it up," it went through my head and it got hotter than it already was.

Amazingly quickly, I prevented her from turning away by increasing the pressure on my lower abdomen. With my hand on her chest, I pressed her to me and laid it down the other around her chin.

"Stay!" I hissed, staring at her .

"Nothing happens that you don't want," I whispered more gently.

This was really the full truth. I would never have thought of doing violence to another person, let alone one, this woman.

Apparently that was said so convincingly or she read it in my eyes despite her horror. Maybe she just wanted to believe it, because like me, maybe she wasn't clear anymore.

In any case, the expression on her face took on gentle features again. However, her gaze again had this indefinable mixture, which could express desire, dream or humility.

Hopefully I didn't dream. I had never seen anything like it before. I could hardly think clearly. I was only excited by the unexpected situation, excited by the sexual tension and euphoric by their trust.

Again I had to / wanted / allowed to kiss her, but started on her cheek, covered her eye with gentle kisses and let me lead her through her nose to her mouth. There I was expected, greeted, taken in as I would not have expected after this abrupt interruption.

Her bottom also showed me that it should go on. This time she pressed against me and moved up and down.

"Just not too strong, otherwise I won't hold out much longer," I thought realistically, because I hadn't relieved my pressure for a day or two.

This is not the only reason why I put my hands back in. Once again, twice, three times or more on the back, breasts, neck and waist, I made room for a kiss on the shoulder blades, licked the spine and kissed the back of my neck until I felt goose bumps. I still don't know whether her body, her scent, her closeness to her or her pride in excitement almost made me lose control. In any case, it started to pull treacherously in my sack, so I started to move in the same rhythm as her.

The rough fabric of her dress also prevented the high of the intoxication. Since the glans had already left the foreskin protection, this textile tormented me a little.

I immediately saw a need for action. So I took my hands off her back, out of her dress and put her on her hips. So I could have reduced our friction to a tolerable level. "If so, because already" I thought to myself. So I relieved some of her pressure by holding on to her and pulled back a little. So I was able to push her dress up a little. It wasn't much necessary, because I already had In addition, the slit in the dress, which I noticed in the hallway when I tried to catch up with it, was already appearing, creating more reserve and moving my hands slightly to the side were one and a dark panties appeared.

I immediately reduced the distance to zero. I almost went back, the fabric felt so cool despite our heated body. It felt so smooth and soft, just blissful. What I had had to "suffer" before was forgotten and immediately made up again umpteen times.

This packaging was also dreamlike like the bra. About half of her cheeks were packed, soon less because I rubbed my cock in her furrow again and thus more material Next to it the fair skin was visible.

The view was not good because we were (luckily still undetected) under the basement stairs in the gloom.

Therefore, a control with the sensitive fingertips was essential. Both hands were now working on their thighs. Up to the panties, then back a little forward. Oh, that felt good. They discovered the transition from the leg to the buttocks, the outer half of the cheek and the place where the panties disappeared into the groin. They also glided over the fine fabric, although I didn't care whether it was expensive silk or cheap plastic. I almost overexcited myself when I accidentally delicately stroked my cock upwards to take care of her back over her cross.

As a result of this action, she was almost bared downstairs. When I became aware of this, I was already at the limit of the final. A pull and rumble on my tail root were clear signs of it, not to mention my feelings of happiness.

On the way back I wanted to conquer new terrain again. My hands found her breasts and stiff nipples unchanged. My mouth caressed my cheek and ear again. But soon I only got to the crook of my neck because my hands had already become independent and were already on her stomach. Everyone wanted to be the first and discover whether the front side of the panties and the bra were worked.

There it was already. My heart jumped for joy or pounded in the neck and filled my cock even more than my idea came true.

And suddenly everything happened very quickly. Caught by my joy, I noticed her movement came. I went down with one hand and reached a noticeable pubic mound, noticed how it was getting tighter, warmer and wetter.

Then I felt something between us. I felt her cool hand run over my glans once or twice and it was all about me.

I just pressed myself against her or she against me. One hand on her pubic, the other on her stomach I shot several times. Then I felt nothing at all, felt another tremor in her stomach and gasped at her.

We both don't know how long I had fainted with her.

Back in consciousness I looked at her, noticed her tear and felt that I would not wake up from this dream without a kiss. Anita seems to be no different.

Then we return to this world. She moved her hand on my only semi-rigid cock. At the same time we noticed how wet and slippery it was there.

"Sorry," I whisper. She shook her head and breathed, "Thank you."

I slowly released her and wanted to reach for the handkerchief. She noticed it, looked me in the eye and said: "I want to keep everything!"

I felt the same. But I could only pull back and sniff her scent on my fingers while I watched her massage my juice into my panties , then smelled on the hand, licked it once and then dried it on the front of the panties.

This almost brought tears to my eyes. It was a sign of closeness and trust that I didn't think possible after such a short time. I stopped supplying my cock to cuddle her again. Then I closed my pants while she rolled her eyes, trying to stuff her breasts into the bra. That was certainly not easy with the constellation of clothes. When I stepped behind her to help her, I saw for a moment the mess I had put on my cross and panties. But had to let go of it to close the bra.

"You're definitely more adept at opening," she remarked. There was nothing to say about that. I preferred to apologize for it with a few kisses on the back.

She made up for it by pulling the dress back down and waving her ass so incomparably artless and sexy that I just had to stroke it again before pulling the zipper up.

Without saying a word, we agreed that this had to be the end of this escapade and kissed each other again.

She was the first to say what had to follow and should be decisive for our future: "Will we see each other again?" "Yes, as soon as possible", was all I got out.

I looked for a business card from my wallet and asked: "Will you give me yours too?" She took one out of her pocket and said: "I have to go".

After a long kiss, she turned and went up the stairs. I just stopped enjoying her movements and smiled and kissed her as she turned again.

The experiment: from soft to hard

"Ok, no problem. See you next week! "I closed the phone and looked at it for a short while.

It was Friday afternoon, one of the most beautiful summer days of the year. The sun glittered from the sky, catching every life on the streets of the city and almost bringing it to a standstill. The air was still.

The call came as a surprise, and it upset my afternoon schedule, at least for a short time. That means that he actually freed me from the somewhat annoying obligation to have a long-standing cooperation conversation with a few young people. They wanted to bring in their web design skills and connect them with my work as a management consultant abroad. Now the boys had canceled or postponed the meeting until next week; they had something important to finish today.

The more I thought about it, the more an inner contentment and serenity spread. Unexpected breaks are actually a godsend, especially on such a perfect day. The city is at its most beautiful when it is half-deserted, or at least when life has a pulse or two. Just like this Friday.

At 8:00 p.m. I announced myself to a friend: chatting, sitting together, having a drink and simply enjoying the evening. That was in five hours. I rarely had so much time to myself. And I started to enjoy the unexpected twist of the day more and more.

"Just having five hours and without the slightest obligation - somehow awesome!" I was happy. Three things manifested themselves almost simultaneously in my brain and hung in the air expectantly: espresso, magazines and outstretched feet. That screamed for implementation .

at the kiosk I bought two magazines, in combination, probably unique in this day "adventure & travel" and "brand eins": wide world meets unconventional economic Just right at this moment..

Less than three minutes later, I was sitting slightly elevated above the sidewalk in a small, cozy cafe and wisely draped myself around the three-legged tables. A nice look at the service, a friendly order and a fourth thing had already manifested itself: a martini, white, with ice cubes. If pleasure, then with style.

Stir sugar into the coffee, open the travel magazine, sip the martini and sort out the outstretched legs: I must have given the great picture of a Friday idler. At least my appearance was almost convincing: sunglasses in my long hair, 3-day beard, sand-colored linen shirt and wide, airy pants. With the selection of drinks on my table, the Italian feeling was almost perfect.

I delved into the report of an adventurous group in the Libyan desert about the sand dune odyssey and was just stuck in a giant dune with the participants when suddenly there was movement in the oppressive heat of the cafe. According to the voices, two women sat behind me. They talked animatedly, but strangely, in an almost whispering tone.

I turned back to my travel report and the sheets of sand - at least until I was startled by a loud order: "Two espresso and two Martini Bianco, with ice cream, please."

The voice was pleasant and when I ordered it I was inevitably reminded of my table. I picked up the martini, eyed it against the dim light in the semi-darkness of the cafe, and slowly put it on.

"Well, get it!" It sounded from behind - determined, but not binding. Kind of nice. I turned slightly, toasted unobtrusively and smiled. Not bad.

The two women were probably in their mid-thirties , and absolutely handsome. Blond, proper and with a cheeky smile the left, brunette, slim and with a deep look the other, both in skirts, dressed in summer, not overly made up and very pleasantly normal, which is rather the exception these days.

The sheets of sand: Somehow the Libyan expedition had to get their car up and running again. That was probably not so easy. Neither was it easy to concentrate on the magazine again during the lively conversation that started again behind me.

"I tell you, it works. I am absolutely certain. There are some special steps that make it possible. "

" Oh come on, you don't believe that yourself. Who told you that? "

"I admit it is a bit unusual, but it is based on a special technique. You can override the blood supply mechanism, sure! "

" Have you tried this before? "

"No, not really yet. I tried it once and it worked so well. I hadn't found the right place to press either. But now I know exactly where it is! "

The drinks of the two women came, glasses clinked and after a short pause the whispered conversation resumed its original journey. No thought to read in peace. I leaned back and waited for the things that the two of them still wanted to say. Another sip of martini.

"So again, you say that the man with your 'technique'", she involuntarily spoke a little quieter, "comes to orgasm, although he does not is stiff? So he cums with a soft cock? "

"If I tell you - that's exactly what I mean! Watch out: after a period of excitement, the tail slackens. Then you have to find the right point at the bottom and press firmly. At the same time, you continue gently at the front. And that also leads to the injection, even if the tail does not become hard again. "She paused

briefly." And that must be incomparably beautiful, much deeper.
"

"And where did you get this tip from?" There was a slightly ironic undertone in the question.

"This is an Indian technique, is probably a variant of the Kamasutra. Monika told me that, she probably did that with her lovers and that with resounding success. "

I involuntarily turned around. I looked into two large, surprised pairs of eyes, which almost fixed me in consternation. I happily turned the martini glass in my hand.

"Aha ..." My slightly amused facial expression spoke volumes. I cleared my throat. "Even if I had wanted to, I couldn't have missed your conversation - we're too close to each other for that. Interesting theory."

I smiled, and that caused them to crawl out of their brief stiffness. The blonde caught herself first, I could tell from her voice that she had dragged on the theory: "Well, if you've already listened to everything, tell us why you are grinning so mockingly? Why should not that work?"

Interesting question. I thought for a moment. "I can't explain anatomically exactly why that is not possible, that is not my profession. But if I can speak from personal experience, that's simply not possible. "

The blonde smiled." Unimaginable, but possible. Otherwise you could rule it out, right? "

1-0 for them. Maybe it wasn't a good idea after all that I got involved in the conversation. But somehow I just had to do it.

"Ok, I can't imagine it. But then please tell me how that should be possible? "

The two women exchanged brief looks. A nod of approval, barely noticeable, came from the brunette.

"Then it might be better if you came to our table with your drinks - otherwise we would discuss this topic with the whole restaurant in five minutes."

The restaurant was almost empty, but there was something convincing about her reasoning. I moved Somehow the whole thing promised to be funny. I had nothing on my unexpectedly free Friday afternoon. A polemic discussion with two cheeky women about male orgasms - why not.

The blonde was Manuela, the brunette introduced herself as Tanja. There were no other social niceties to get to know each other and I hardly had time to examine the degree of femininity of my two new table mates when Manuela began bluntly with her explanation of the male sexual processes.

"It's just about stopping the blood supply once the tail has become limp. The excitement can still be maintained, or at least quickly restored. And then everything goes its usual way - only that the tail is then soft. "

Her directness fascinated me. She was convinced of what she said and made it known. No matter whether we were in a cafe and we had introduced us only two minutes ago, gorgeous, and logically flawless.

I tried to contradict anyway. "Never when a man gets aroused will the cock become stiff. Period. Otherwise, it may be nice, but the arousal is never like that big that it could lead to orgasm. "

I felt watched by both women as I defended my point. It was as if they were looking me over, as if I were in an exam. Something in me was gripped by a certain unrest. I was trying to turn the tables when Manuela started to answer. "If you get the right pressure points, you can separate the two things. Just like orgasm and ejaculation are actually two different things that usually only happen together. "

Miss Dr. med. Sex had full lips and an attractive, beautifully curved face. The blue eyes radiated joy of life, between snow-white teeth and the lightly made-up lips she brought out her words with full conviction. Her opulent upper body rose and fell in support of her statements, and a promising neckline allowed a playful insight into the hidden. With beautifully groomed, red fingernails, she finally stroked her long curls and looked at me challenging.

I turned to Tanja. "What do you think about this whole topic?"

A short surprise was reflected on her narrow, pointed lips, which was immediately replaced by an open smile. Dark eyes revealed depth, laugh lines played around her warm mouth. The slightly bitter touch combined wonderfully with her soft voice. A suggestive look opened my eyes. "Well, I don't really believe in it. But I know Manuela, if she wasn't absolutely convinced, then she wouldn't tell. "

Her eyes slid and slowly floated over to her blonde friend. She smiled a little wider." Right?

I felt that something had passed me at that moment, something that had passed me smoothly.

I pulled my remaining espresso towards me and held on to it. A nervousness grew in me, which I tried to cover up with further arguments. "But still, that can't work - I've never heard of anything like that."

While Tanja slowly turned her face back to me, Manuela looked at me directly and openly. "You really seem to be very convinced of yours Position." She paused briefly, just the right number of nanoseconds. "Would you like to try it out?"

The time, which passed at a snail's pace anyway, stopped.

Manuela gave me a challenging look. Tanja eyed me with a smile, lovingly.

Both were obviously waiting for an answer from me. To do this, the words and their meaning had to be processed in my brain twists. It took time. And I have my last sip of martini.

Manuela also raised her glass. "If you are convinced that it doesn't work anyway, you have nothing to lose, do you?" She smiled, mysterious and feminine. At that moment she seemed to bloom in her femininity. Her facial features softened, almost like that she wanted to take me in with it.

I came back to life. cleared my throat. looked around. tried to look cool. and then croaked: "How, right now?"

Manuela and Tanja looked at each other, nodded and smiled and agreed. "Yes," I said in unison.

Tanya put her warm hand on my arm. "Or are you going to do something better ...?"

I looked at her and could only shake my head. I was exhausted. These two women, whom I had only known for a quarter of an hour, wanted my cock for one trying out new technology. To prove something to myself and myself. So an experiment.

"So an experiment?" I asked into our small group, which suddenly seemed very intimate.

Again this smile from Manuela, but a little softer this time. "So to speak. You say it doesn't work and I want to try anyway. Let's see what comes out. You could call that an experiment. "

At that moment I caught myself again. I started to think. And filed claims. "Yes, and what if it - which I am assuming - doesn't work? Then what did I gain? "

An amused look change followed. The two seemed to really like the game. Tanja looked at me, her hand moved playfully on my arm." Well, if two women are trying to get your cock, that's all unexpected, that's certainly not the worst thing on a summer Friday afternoon, is it? "

She looked at me cheekily, almost demanding, while an enjoyable smile played on her lips. "And what has arisen after that, we haven't talked about yet ..." She left the sentence unfinished and thus achieved the intended, perfectly timed effect.

I melted like a chocolate ice cream on the sidewalk in the midday heat.

With my heart pounding and my blood pressure very high, I forced myself not to completely lose my maintenance. Stressed out I fished for my wallet, put 20 euros on the table in slow motion (to take a breath), reached for my magazines and got up.

"Is it far from here?" I asked in the most casual tone that my automatic speech center was able to produce.

The action at least brought me out of the lagging position. Manuela and Tanja got up and I stopped They opened the door for them, of course, just so that at least now I could get a good view of the two graces who were just dragging me so insolently.

Manuela was all woman, firm and buxom, a full woman. Light complexion, wide knee skirt in washed purple, plus a mauve blouse, under which the straps of her enormous bra emerged. Tanja was a little more delicate, but the curves in the right places, which was particularly noticeable due to her light linen trousers. A great bubble butt, and she knew how to put it in scene. Fortunately, both were stylish enough not to let their elegant legs end in cheap slippers.

The two were a direct hit. I was ready to play with her no matter how far it went. I had time and it was Friday afternoon. And it was summer.

Manuela went ahead and tried to make conversation about the weather as a matter of course. You could see that she was excited too - probably not an action she or Tanja did every day! It was fine with me, because apart from making my cock available for this 'experiment', no expectations were placed on me at first.

The thought made me swallow a lot and I suddenly became aware of the absurdity of the situation. I followed two women to their apartment to answer the question of discussion with my own cock, whether orgasm with a soft cock would be possible. HI?!?!

Incomprehensible. But when I looked up, the two women were still walking forward along the sidewalk, turning right, and coming to a stop in front of an imposing house entrance. "And, still there?"

I grinned. "But of course - I'm really looking forward to it ..." The bulge in my pants had already reached impressive dimensions by then - but that's exactly what Manuela wanted to take care of. I decided to just enjoy the performance and everything else and started climbing the stairwell. Wonderful coolness enveloped us when we entered the apartment. I pulled the door shut.

"Water?" Came around the corner, and we all met in the spacious dining kitchen. Everyone tried to arrange the upcoming events for themselves in silence. A brief hint of shyness was passed over with amused laughter.

By now, Manuela was barely there Nervousness visible. Tanja was more careful there, the matter was a little more mysterious, wicked, insecure. Her face glowed with the slight blush that had risen in her. While our eyes met, lost in depth and the tension of the Situation came in small sparks, Manuela approached me from behind. She grabbed my butt with both hands.

"Wow, that is crunchy. It feels really good." Her hands were moving. "And how is that further up ...?"

While Tanja was standing opposite me and holding my gaze, Manuela grabbed me from behind and grabbed my tail directly. He stood stiff and hard in my pants, allowing it to be stroked slowly but skillfully through the fabric. I got lost in the brown eyes that opened completely.

"Hmmm, wonderful ..." I heard it behind me. Then the tone changed and the magic of the moment was briefly interrupted. "We're going to the bedroom, aren't we?"

Off, march, our troop started to move. Manuela was hardly afraid of contact - and if she did, at least she didn't show it. Slightly undecided about the sequence of the steps to follow, I sat on the bed that stood in the middle of the room. Stylish furnishings, sand-colored with a touch of turquoise, and the airy decoration gave the room a weightless ambience. The heat of the day lurked in front of the open window, but didn't dare to enter. The air was pleasant and cozy.

"Then let's see the toys!" Manuela called with almost exaggerated cheer into the expectant silence that had formed between us. Since she started, I didn't want to stand behind. But I didn't miss my two teammates for a second We undressed at a proper distance, each one for

myself . I was completely caught up in the absurd situation of undressing in a bedroom with two almost unknown women so that they could perform an orgasm experiment on my cock My rod stood upright like a steel pipe in the air when I stripped off my pants, the shirt followed immediately, and standing naked in the room I watched my appetizing companions.

Tanja's body presented a seamless tan. As suspected, she was rather slim, but with distinctive curves: firm apple buttocks with a lovely anthracite-colored slit, soft hips, only the slight beginning of a bulging belly and heavenly breasts that protruded small and pointed.

Manuela was pretty much the opposite: voluminous, plump tits, flesh on the hips, strong thighs and an opulent ass - and all so properly held by fair skin that she gave the wonderful picture of a thoroughbred woman.

I sucked in the air and enjoyed the moment. My cock protruded pulsating and I saw myself exposed to an optical pattern. There was nothing to hide for me: the long hair on the shoulder, well-proportioned body, athletic figure and a smooth-shaved, even genitals. The two women also seemed to take note of this, because with their appreciative looks they probably praised themselves for the good choice of their examination subject.

"Great," I thought, too, and grabbed left and right to get a tit in my hand. Both were warm and soft, slightly aroused, and the fast heartbeat was noticeable underneath. Manuela grabbed the object again without hesitation Her main interest. She touched my cock with an expert grip, carefully felt my eggs, scratched my testicles. She familiarized herself. Then she pulled the foreskin back to the stop and jerked me a few times. She was obviously satisfied.

"You are beautiful, very masculine." She smiled at me. "Perfect for our experiment."

Tanja said nothing, enjoying the scene with fading uncertainty. Of course she was there in her nudity. I had to look down at her involuntarily and came across a small piece of grass made of dark pubic hair that was enthroned over her gender entrance. Below was smooth skin, and the entrance to their paradise. Simply loved.

Tanja accompanied my optical excursions with a playful smile. She knew exactly what treasure was between her legs. But she made no move to issue an invitation or the like.

For that, Manuela became more active. She led me, my cock in firm grip, to the bed. "Make yourself comfortable with the pillows, the best thing is that you put something on, then you can see everything."

I had no choice but to follow this request. So I sat upright on the top of the bed, a pillow in the back. I spread my legs so that my stiff tube was pointing straight up. The two women made themselves comfortable in front of it: Tanja at a distance, but close to my left leg; Manuela closer to the action so that my leg came to rest between her thighs. It was hot and wet.

On the outside, however, she was not noticeable, she remained completely neutral. "Now I'm also excited myself, but I'm sure that it will work. A nice cock! "

With this praise, she grabbed my braces and went to work. She knew very well what she was doing. Boldly, she began to scratch my balls with her long, red fingernails, gently and constantly. The other hand gripped the root of my tail and exerted rhythmic pressure there. It felt great.

Tanya took turns looking at what was happening between my legs and my eyes. Her eyes were deep and increasingly lustful. She cleverly hid her own sex, but her hand on my thigh expressed active well-being.

Slowly Manuela jerked herself warm on my rock hard rod. She definitely increased my arousal. The acorn took on an increasingly darker color and became more plump. A slight pull began to announce my lumbar area. My lust grew. She did it extremely well.

Manuela went to work concentrated. She was obviously determined to use her entire repertoire, that is part of her plan. I should be fine, I enjoyed the attention and the certainty that I would still get cumshot on this bed one afternoon or the other. At that point it seemed to me rather questionable whether it would go as Manuela imagined. My stiffener poked excitedly into the afternoon.

"Well, now it won't be long with the hosing down if I go on like this, is it?" Manuela smiled knowingly at me. She had been interpreted masterfully and the increasing pulsation in my balls. With her sober, almost distant manner Working my cock had brought me to a climax in a very short time, but now she took her hands away.

"Now comes perhaps the most difficult part of the afternoon: we have to let your handsome cock go limp again ..." laughed cheerfully at this statement and I agreed. She could be right about that again. But we had time and were relaxed enough.

I tried conversation and asked the two about professional activities. While Manuela organized and managed marketing events, Tanja had a boutique nearby. Actually, she should have returned there after the coffee break, but she left the sale to her employee and herself in the afternoon. A wonderful concept.

I told about the desert trip that I had previously read in the cafe and spread a few stories from my own trips to Arabia. And what seemed completely unthinkable shortly before actually worked over time: in a situation in which I was lying in bed with two naked, attractive women, my cock became soft again and retreated to normal size.

We noticed all three of them almost simultaneously and looked down. He slept gently and almost innocently between my legs. A drop of advance juice had formed and shone from the top. Otherwise, he was completely relaxed and peaceful. A wonder.

Manuela reacted immediately and went back to work before any natural reaction could start again. She grabbed my completely unprepared member and knowingly duped it. Below my testicles, somewhere on the way back, she pressed a finger firmly in the side. She did the same trick above my tail, right where the limb grows from the pubic bone.

"This is how I stop the blood supply, but the arousal mechanism is still going on. So all the prerequisites for a sparkling end remain intact. "Frau Professor smiled at her work with satisfaction and held this death grip with one hand for my best piece. Nothing moved.

That alone brought my excitement back." Now you have So I'm in complete control - that's how you like it, right? " I smiled. "But you haven't proven anything yet and won nothing. What's next? "

Manuela let out a rolling hum as a sign of her increased well-being. Her thighs hugged my leg more closely, and I got an even more intense sense of her excitement. Her soft, meaty pussy seemed to be on fire. "Your cock is beautiful even in this state." She took it in her hand. It was a strange sight to see him so vulnerable and soft between her fingers. But it was also exciting. A new dimension seemed to be around us to grow.

Tanja watched the new development with great interest. She had put a hand down between her legs and was rubbing lightly against it. The soft tail seemed to fuel her interest almost more than the previous stiff version. Full of anticipation, she beamed at me with her big, fawn eyes. Her mouth was slightly open and her lips were wet.

Manuela took the next step. "You feel great, so gentle and soft. Let's see what you say about it. "Without loosening the grip, she touched my tail with the other hand. She put her thumb directly under the glans, in my most sensitive area, and began to rotate swiftly. Her index finger enclosed me from above and acted as a counterpart, exerting a gentle pressure that steadily increased.

Whether I wanted it or not, my excitement grew again. It was a different, more subtle kind of arousal than I was used to from before. I felt their movements deeper, they penetrated me more and in a more comprehensive way.

The condition of my tail did not change in any way. It stayed soft. Manuela increased the pressure at the two points again, and that did not fail to have an effect: no blood could pass, and my cock remained limp. I was thrilled.

"Do you see what I told you?" She cried triumphantly, increasing the intensity of her rotation below my glans. "It works!"

I tried to put her hasty triumph into perspective. "Yeah, well, it doesn't get stiff, but that doesn't mean that I get to orgasm.

She looked me in the eye with the feeling of a sure winner. "Look at me, handsome man: I'll give you a maximum of five more minutes and then your juice will flow out of this flaccid cock."

This brutally clear announcement fueled me again. I noticed that something was brewing in my lumbar region, but I couldn't define it, it was a new, unknown feeling. The blood shot into my head and also stimulated me. It got serious.

"That's real, you really make him splash!" Tanja had suddenly awakened from her trance and was now actively intervening. She was blown away by what was happening before her eyes.

"Oh yes, it won't be long now, I can feel it." Manuela was now fully in her element. "Come on, help, then it will be even hotter! Scratch his balls!"

Without hesitation Tanja did as she was told and for the first time I felt her hands. She moved a little closer to draw furrows over my contracted testicles with my fingernails. She was definitely scratching my most sensitive skin and getting it going.

In an unbelievable way, the two managed to put my soft cock in an almost disturbing excitement. It was completely beyond me what was going on between my legs. I had never experienced something so intense and crazy. Still the same picture: my rod, which previously stood stiffly and evenly upwards, lay softly and innocently in the hands of this woman who worked the head with rhythmic certainty. And it does it infinitely well.

The pull in my abdomen increased. Any muscles in my butt started to contract. My breath grew faster.

"There is no such thing!" I exclaimed with joyful horror, and almost at the same time I let out a small cry: a surge of electricity was suddenly whipped through my body.

I looked down at the incredible scenery that presented itself to me: Manuela held my soft cock tightly and massaged my glans with glowing enthusiasm. Her breath came intermittently, so excited the situation. Tanja stared spellbound at my cock; her scratching deep below my balls became even more intense. The two were preparing for this grand finale before.

In the meantime it was clear to me that it would not be long in coming. My cock didn't show the slightest bit. Manuela had him under perfect control. For that it started to twitch in my balls. Tanja acknowledged this activity with a delighted shout. Manuela started to moan herself and intensified her efforts for me again.

A familiar throbbing started in my back. I was stunned. The two were about to bring me to orgasm, with a limp cock! I groaned as another twitch went through my body. With my eyes wide open I didn't let my lumbar region slip out of sight, I didn't want to miss anything from this event.

My eggs started to fidget, then they bounced. They performed an unprecedented dance, completely independent and disconnected from my cock. The rhythmic pulsation had now caught my entire butt and abdomen. I could feel every single contraction, and it went through me vehemently. Still, I tried to keep my body as still as possible. It got even more violent.

The heralds of my own orgasm whipped me like blows and drove the beads of sweat onto my forehead. Every muscle started to tighten and my abdomen grew hard like a board - except for the tail, which remained in its same, soft state. I felt the heat wave rise inside me. It was so far.

"That doesn't exist !!!" I shouted into the afternoon when I was still desperately trying to defend myself against the superiority of the first wave. It was in vain. An orgasm completely unexpected in this form broke and I surrendered me in the ultimate tenderness of my two wonderful tormentors. I was just run over.

"It comes, it comes!" Manuela's triumphal shouts came from afar to my ear. With her mouth open and a groan pressed, Tanja pressed her nails into my twitching eggs one last time. Then something exploded in my stomach and a huge electric shock hit my entire body. I felt a waterfall collect inside me and storm to the exit. I desperately forced my eyes to stay open.

The first ray that wound through my soft tail and found the exit appeared infinite. He flowed tight and firm out of me - it was not a firm shot, but rather an elongated pull. Manuela gasped loudly with joy as the whitish liquid poured over her hand. And that was just the beginning.

Beam after beam, inexplicable amounts of my semen poured from the depths of my body. My soft tail became an outlet for the pent-up heat and lust of the day. Over and over again my balls contracted and pressed the juice outside. Every time a twinkling bliss of joy tortured my body and I writhed under the sweet torments of orgasm. I kept desperately silent so as not to let the incomparability of the moment end prematurely - I never wanted to stop squirting my hot juice as a reward for these two love angels.

It trembled again and again in me, and only slowly did the intensity of the climax decrease again. The juice was still dripping from my cock, and the stroking hands had long been bathed in a sea of ??seeds. They also couldn't get enough of it, they kept stimulating me, stroking, caressing, scratching and stimulating, until finally the uncontrolled twitching of my eggs subsided.

For moments I was completely unable to show any kind of reaction. Completely exhausted and with a blurry look I looked down at the paradisiacal mess. I had injected more than ever in my life. And I had climaxed like never before.

Manuela loosened her grip. She looked up at me briefly, and our eyes met in a dimension of deep satisfaction. Then she smeared my juice over my sex and gently stroked every inch of my slippery skin.

"Incredible, that was really super cool!" She seemed very satisfied with herself and her work. She looked at me again. "And you went off like a rocket." She smiled.

Tanja now seemed to have recovered from the events. She was awesome, you could tell that from her look. She brought my semen to her breast and playfully circled her nipple.

"Wow - that was unbelievable!" I said, exhausted. "What did you do to me there? A whole new dimension has opened up there!"

Slowly I could see clearly again. The shadowy perception fell away from me and my brain functioned at least reasonably normal. The pictures of my semen, which had poured out into freedom through the flaccid tail, still stuck, like Pattex in my head. Thanks to Manuela's new stimulation method, the orgasm had probably looked for another, deeper path and manifested itself in me. Everything had almost taken part in the climax - only my cock was as if not involved in the whole.

In a moment of sudden clarity, I noticed what was wrong with that afternoon's picture. "Yes, and what should I do with my sucked cock now? Should it stay that way? "

Four eyes looked at me. Down between my legs, then up again. There was no response.

"Now you've got all the valuable juice out of me, and should it just soak into the sheets? Wouldn't that be a shame? "I tried to put a certain impatience in my voice. Somewhere I was right - at least I persuaded myself.

The two looked at me first, then at each other. Even Manuela had a short speech You could literally see how it rattled and worked in their heads. Either they would throw me out right now or they would give me a good kick first. It would be well deserved.

Manuela leaned forward briefly and looked at me Then she put my cock in her mouth.

The suddenness of this movement made me shiver. I kept silent as a mouse while she started licking the semen from my cock. Eager, she sucked on my skin and even tried to get the cock together with the eggs in her mouth. She managed for a brief moment. Then my cock started to grow.

My hand reached for her - and met gold. The gap between her legs opened wetly. With no resistance, I slid my fingers deep into their grotto.

As always, Tanya was a bit more reserved. But then she clearly drew attention to herself. She gently pushed Manuela aside and put herself in a good position. She hotly took my cock between her lips.

Rowing wildly in Manuela's cunt with my fingers, I enjoyed an unforgettable moment. While one sucked my cock in her mouth, the other licked my balls clean. They didn't want to waste anything. My loins almost collided. And in the midst of this mini-orgy, my cock woke up again.

He grew deep between Tanja's lips. He grew up and became stiff. Tanja's eyes widened at the unexpected filling. She tried to put everything in her mouth. None of us had expected this development. Manuela looked up in disbelief and then grabbed my cock root, as if to make sure it was real: less than five minutes after the last, the 'soft' orgasm, I was rock hard.

I felt new energy rise in me. My loins, still completely exhausted a few moments ago, moved powerfully. My hand went deeper into the dripping pussy. Manuela moaned with her eyes closed, my cock in hand. Tanya sucked the acorn into herself. It was maddening. I had to prevent that.

With my free hand I touched Tanja gently on the cheek. She looked up at me.

"Come here," I said softly. Unbridled lust spoke from her eyes. She let go of my cock and straightened up. With my free hand I grabbed her column. Wet.

I had to fuck her.

We both knew what would happen , yes had to happen. Willig lay down beneath me and spread her legs. My cock was now stiff, ready to attack. I did not know how he would cope with this burden - but his well-being was absolutely secondary in this case.

I came across. I slid forward. I entered. Received from the heat, I was about to spray directly. I ignored the signals from my body and started to fuck Tanya. I didn't take my hand out of Manuela's cunt.

It was a pleasure to penetrate them. She was ready and she was awesome - which was no wonder after the audition. She had now put aside her shy manner. She wrapped her legs around me, clawed her fingernails into my butt and pulled me deep inside. The force of our movements ended in a loud clap. I was in her for a long time.

Manuela had slipped slightly to one side and lay there ecstatic. With one hand on her clit, she started rubbing wildly. I wedged my hand in her pussy and clawed into her. Violent moans announced her near orgasm.

Tanja had slipped into the active role below me and rhythmically pressed her pelvis against mine. My pipe slipped out before it disappeared into the depths of her femininity. The friction on my tail was the ultimate aphrodisiac for me, which I had not previously been granted. The only way to explain why I was almost ready to come again.

Beside us, Manuela flinched and cried out her lust. Her pelvis sucked my hand in and milked the welcome intruder in wild greed. So that was done - and it scared me.

Tanja was also about to lose herself. She pumped my cock inside her, and her movements became more focused and hectic. Her gentle, friendly features had been paired with passion and reflected the epitome of unbridled femininity. It was wonderful to be ridden by her in this form. For a moment I saw the situation from an observer's perspective and could feel everything at the same time: the sun, the heat, the afternoon, the air, the tension, the passion, the greed, the smell and the sex.

I was in the last twitch. I pulled my hand out of Manuela's cunt and threw myself on Tanja. I rammed my pipe hard into her, speared her, drilled myself into her. I met a soft resistance deep in it - I had reached the end. We paused and she looked at me with abysmal, unrestrained lust. At the same time, the muscles of her pussy contracted violently around my cock. Once, twice, and a third time.

Then she let out a long, drawn-out scream and rammed her pelvis up to the ultimate finale, towards me. That was the end of me. I easily adapted to the rhythm and surrendered to her muscle twitches. Again a load of semen pressed through my tube, this time to pour into Tanja's innermost femininity. I was deep in her and let myself be carried away by the intensity of our orgasm.

Tanya came deep and violent, she never let go of me. Despite the slow decay, my cock twitched in her. But even Tanja always wriggled a little at the slightest movement that I made on and in her. We were wedged into each other and delivered to each other in the waves of our climax. Finally, an almost imperceptible tremor ran up her body and mine down again. We felt like one. And completely emptied.

Tired, but with sparkling eyes, Manuela lay next to us. She had noticed our last twitches and had her own joy with it. She reached out and lightly stroked her friend's cheek. The eyes of the two women met and there was nothing but blissful contentment in them - and I could only agree with that.

And all of this happened so completely unexpectedly on a free, summer Friday afternoon.

The End.

The Glade

Today is actually a normal Sunday. I got up shortly after sunrise, relaxed and had a good breakfast. Bread, coffee, a few small tomatoes. Only the egg, I'm going to save that today because I want to go running straight away and it really doesn't go well. Then I scurry a bit through the apartment. There have been a lot of problems in the past week. I also have to digest the food at least a little bit before I set off

I live close to an extensive forest with many paths that are great for jogging. So I change my clothes and slip on my new running shoes. The old woman was just down. It is not far to the forest and so I easily start walking when I have left the house. The weather is perfect today. Slightly over 20 degrees but slightly cloudy so that it doesn't get too hot. Things are going well today. I'm pretty quick and for once I don't hurt anything.

Still something starts to bother me. Maybe I should have had a quick pee beforehand. How stupid. At kilometer 5 I notice that it is no longer possible. I better go to the bushes somewhere. But where? Everything is so clearly visible here and there is a lot going on in the forest. I have already met 10 joggers. Not to mention the dog owners. Then it occurs to me that a piece of somewhat denser fir forest is coming and there is a small clearing in the middle. I should be unobserved there.

So a few minutes later I hit the tall dark trees. I like the place, it seems a little magical. Then the clearing that I had in my head appears before me. I look around quickly, meanwhile it is quite urgent. So I take my cock out of my pants, which is pretty easy with running gear and relax. Ah, that's good for you!

Suddenly I hear a sound that doesn't belong here. It comes from the clearing. I try to stop, but it's already too late. I see a pretty woman sit up out of the tall grass in the clearing and look me straight in the eye. It is only a few meters away. Man is embarrassed. And even more so when she looks down at me and smiles as she looks more closely at my cock. Fortunately, I'm finally done and of course I want to pack up right away.

But she looks at me and shakes her head. I stop and consider what that should be now. She visibly jerks and gets up. I am amazed when I see that she has pushed up her skirt and is not wearing any laundry underneath. Her cunt is completely shaved, I can see that even from this distance. It looks plump. Her labia seem to be swollen. A pretty sight that makes my balls tingle. At that moment it occurs to me again that I am standing there with my bare cock and of course she now sees that he is getting hard. What to do?

She takes the decision from me and waves me over to her. I hesitate, but then think that I have nothing to lose and go to her. When I stand in front of her, I want to say something. I don't know exactly yet, but I don't get to it because she puts a finger on my lips and shows me that I should be silent. She grabs my hand and pulls me down into the tall grass. I let it happen. She sits down in front of me and simply lets her bent legs slide apart so that I can now take a closer look at her wonderful cunt.

She is sharp and starts to stroke herself. Her fingers slide up and down her labia until they part and reveal all of her femininity. My cock, still looking out of my running pants, starts to twitch. I free him and take off my pants.

She takes a closer look at me and starts rubbing her cunt more. Her clitoris is the target of her fingers, which also slide into her wet hole again and again. They pull longer and longer threads of moisture behind them when they leave the cave.

Oh man, it looks so sharp that I can't help it. I extend my hand to her, but she immediately rejects it. Not bad, but clearly. She doesn't want to be touched, that much is clear. OK. So I take my cock in hand. Your smile is clear. She likes it. And she starts rubbing her wet cunt harder again. She is concentrating more and more on her small bud, which now looks cheekily out of her small skin fold. Your hole is now wide open.

How I would like to put 2 or 3 fingers in there! Or maybe my cock. But I submit and also start to do it myself. With slow and powerful ups and downs I let my foreskin slide over my plump red acorn. The way I like it. With the other hand I start massaging my eggs. I don't take my eyes off her for a second.

I see her breathing become more violent. I also accelerate my rhythm. Then it happens very quickly. She climaxes and is now completely out of breath. She rubs her clitoris vigorously and quickly. I see her body rear up as she orgasms. Her whole cunt starts to pulsate and with a strong surge she pours her pent-up cunt juice on the blanket on which she is lying.

That is too much for me. I can not anymore! And that's how I come too. My sperm spurted out with powerful bursts. Almost up to her. What an orgasm. My whole body is trembling. And only after the 6th or 7th boost do I start to calm down. I close my eyes briefly to take a deep breath. Then I look at her.

We both smile and know that we should repeat that. She reaches next to her and takes a small piece of paper and a pen out of her pocket and writes down her number for me. She also writes: Next time I want to be fucked. I smile at her and nod. Then we both get dressed again and disappear in different directions after she gave me a quick kiss on the lips. I will probably never forget this experience.

The End.

Barbara

December 4th is Barbara's Day.

I have visited her for years to give her a bouquet of cherry twigs for her name day. No, she was not a strict believer. It was more of a gimmick. Last year, however, the meeting was different than in previous years.

When I arrived in the evening, her apartment was still dark. There was no recognizable reaction to my ringing either. I just thought I heard a thud.

Strange! We had a date. And Barbara was always reliable! Okay, they used the famous academic district often and gladly. But: she was a woman! She was the woman of my dreams! I've been in love with her for twenty years! But I never said or showed it to her!

We went to kindergarten together. At that time she was just one of those "stupid girls" for me. Red-haired, cheeky and played with dolls. Best of all: family. I should always play father then. Man! I thought that was stupid!

In elementary school we only ran side by side, we hardly took any notice of it. That only changed in high school. Suddenly other boys were in trouble here. She was teased because of her red hair. A particularly unpleasant clique had even started physical attacks.

I was not the strongest in our age group, but I was able to defend myself and I was pretty confident, so I almost automatically became their protector.

Over time, whenever she had grief, I became her point of contact. She spoke of me as her "nominal brother". Just as her father's friend was "Uncle Heinz" for her, so she was a "nominal uncle", so I was her "nominal brother".

We were 15 years old when my best friend Thomas discovered that Barbara was a girl, until then she was only a friend of ours, a member of our clique. As a result, she became his girlfriend. And so she was immediately taboo for me, even though I had to find out that I would have liked to be in his place.

We were 22 when the two got married. Of course I was the best man. And still a suggestion box and nominal brother. Thomas was not necessarily one of the most loyal contemporaries. So it happened that my shoulder got soaked quite a few times.

We were 28 when the divorce was pronounced. Thomas went to the Far East as the manager of his company. In the years that followed, his greetings came from Korea, Nepal, Laos and Cambodia. In Laos he married (the Laotian a Laotian!) And had six children. He stayed there. Only letter, email and SMS contact remained.

Barbara moved from the big house in the state capital back to us in the country. Only two houses down my street she found a place to stay. However, the contact was rather sporadic. She seemed to be divorced for years. She wasn't ready for new relationships.

Only my shoulder was still happily used for leaning and moistening.

With her (and mine) now 35 years old she was an absolute beauty. As I said: red-haired! As not yet said: a full woman! Not too slim! But wonderfully rounded! I loved her more than ever. But I still didn't think I had a chance.

No! I was not an Adonis! But she was an Aphrodite! How should that fit!

When I thought of her, I thought in superlatives.

She wore her hair long. Although they were very wavy, they reached in dark copper-red cascades up to their well-shaped bottom. They only ended in the middle of her thighs.

Her bright eyes fascinated me again and again with her intense green. Anyone who didn't think of a tigress had no imagination.

Her full lips were always bright red. I never saw her other than with lipstick. I never met her without actually wanting to kiss her right away.

Her breast was a revelation. I always wondered how you could still walk upright with these mountains. Her chest was so wide that she could still be seen past the upper arms when viewed from behind. Many people, especially women, felt that this was too much of a good thing. But there was nothing better for me than to hold her in my arms (if only to give comfort) and to feel her fullness.

Her waist was very narrow. You almost got the impression that she was wearing a corset. But it was not so.

Her hips were a little wider for that. (That was more inviting for me, though!) Wider than her shoulder girdle. The bottom also had a beautifully pronounced apple shape. And the strength left nothing to be desired.

And then her legs. My God! Her legs!

There are shoe models! There are stocking models! But I've never seen legs like this anywhere else. Well shaped, with slight curves on the calves, with slim bonds that captivated me!

And this length! Barbara was not tall, but her legs reached up to the sky.

Now I had been waiting in front of the door for so long that I was getting cool. And I still heard this strange rumble at irregular intervals.

This house, Barbara lived on the ground floor, had balconies to the rear. I wanted to see if I could see anything. So I went around the building and pulled myself up on the balcony railing to see into the room.

I've crashed many times. Mostly due to alcohol. This time, however, out of sheer laughter. But the sight was too beautiful!

Barbara had told me two weeks ago that after Christmas decorations she had to see what was still needed, what could be thrown away. And now she lay there like a fallen Christmas tree. Decorated all over with fairy lights. She was so caught up in it that she couldn't move. Even two strands of chain ran through her mouth so that she couldn't even call for help.

When I had calmed down a little, I pulled myself up on the balcony and was able to reach the handle of the balcony door through the tilted window.

My comment that such a nicely tied Christmas package made me hungry for a snack made me look angry, but when I first took the chain out of her mouth, I couldn't help it: I had to give her a kiss.

She was so helpless in my arms that I couldn't resist the opportunity. And the kiss quickly became a real kiss! The kiss became very intense! The kiss dragged on! I sank in the kiss! The kiss threatened to swallow me up!

And ...

... uuund ...

... uuuuuunnnnd ...

... the kiss was returned! Barbara kissed ME! It was clear! YOU KISSED ME!

It was only when we were both suffering from acute shortness of breath that I let go of her lips. But I was still holding her in my arms. I hugged her and stammered something like this that I've been waiting for twenty years to never let go of. And similarly confused stuff.

Our mouths were found again and again. Again and again we made each other speechless. I stroked her again and again. Then I carried her to the couch and continued where we had just stopped.

After a little over half an hour, we realized that Barbara was still wrapped up like a roll roast in front of me.

And then she said the most beautiful thing to me! What I would never have dared to dream: "I love you! I have loved you for years! And I think it's nice to be delivered to you so helplessly! "

At this point she didn't lower her voice so that I considered the sentence to be finished. So I ask:" But ...? "

"But it would be nice if you could get rid of me now! Because I have to! "

The evening went on so funny and so beautiful. And it didn't stop there. It became a permanent facility. Today, a year later, we live together and are considering a wedding.

And today, a year later, we both enjoy it when I put a handy package out of it and dedicate myself to the parts of her body that are still accessible. And these are extremely attractive places. But we only wanted to use the fairy lights for the Christmas tree. Our captivating relationship had to be shaped by other means.

The End.

Stage show

It's a hot day. You ordered me to wear a narrow top that just extends over my breasts and a scarf that I tied around my waist. Both are yellow and black, almost like a tiger skin. I only have a thong under the shawl, actually just a triangle, which just covers my pubic area and is held together by two ribbons. You want to show me here today, you said - otherwise I don't know anything.

My eyes are blindfolded and you only take off my bandage when we have reached your destination. It is behind a stage that is brightly illuminated with spotlights. The bright light dazzles me and I can only see the round bright surface on which a black St. Andrew's cross is placed. In the dark room beyond, you can guess the spectators from the murmur. You order me to put a leather cord around my neck, on which there is a leash, hold me tight. We wait and with waiting, my nervousness-mixed desire increases, spreads over the whole body.

A lady enters the stage, all dressed in leather, only the breasts and thighs are free, the face is hidden behind a mask. She is tall, slim and holds a whip in her hand. She announces that a master will show off his big cat, which, on his instructions, will drive a victim from the audience slowly and with all the rules of art to madness. I listen and I realize that I will be one of the actors. It tingles between my legs, my hands get wet.

When the lady asks the question about volunteers in the audience, it gets restless in the audience. Three guys are dragging one of their friends onto the stage. He defends himself vigorously and probably does not agree with his cronies' decision that he should take an active role here. The guys are all about my age, between 20 and 25 years old. The victim is a black-haired boy with half-length, slightly wavy hair and a nice face. He is wearing tight jeans shorts and a t-shirt that has been pushed up by the tug of war with his friends. As he braces himself against it, his leg, arm and abdominal muscles are tense. You can see that he is sporty. His figure, narrow waist and broad upper body,

After the boys have pulled him into the middle of the stage with loud hoots, the lady beckons three figures all in latex. While two are holding him, the third grips him from behind under the armpits, pulls his hands up and presses his head down with his hands. The boy can no longer defend himself, is fixed in the handle. The lady waves to his friends to leave the stage. The two dressed in black push the victim's T-shirt up over their arms, the fidget does nothing to help them. Then, at a further wave, the lady opens his jeans, pushes them down, takes off the Nikes and socks and lets the pants slide off his feet. The boy now only has a narrow pair of panties. How electrified I see the booking, which clearly shows

The lady steps up to him, pulls his head back by the hair, says he should stop fighting back. The hottest experience of his life would be waiting for him now: A female tiger would kill him. The two blacks come back and slide his slip down. The lady grabs the boy between the legs, raises his gender and pulls him once to the left and once to the right to present it to the now roaring audience. Then she pushes him towards St. Andrew's Cross. His two arms are pushed up and fastened to the upper posts in leather bracelets. Then his legs are pulled apart, scratched and tied to the lower ones. The lady reaches again between his legs, weighs the parts in his hand and thinks they will soon be bigger.

My master looks at me. "You know what your job is now - finish it off. He has to go crazy with lust. Take your clothes off, strip, show yourself and your body ... everything ... and then drive him crazy with your body and especially with your tongue. Don't you dare to fail! Now on all fours, cat! I lead you in. "

I obediently let myself be led to the stage by the collar, hissed a few times, sat down on my knees at the signal of my master and turned in all directions. The audience acknowledged it with hoots:" Stripping. ...strip...!!". My master undid the collar and stepped back. I knew what I had to do!

I let myself roll on my back and braced myself with my shoulders and legs, formed a hollow back, raised my legs with my hands, slowly and seductively ... over the inside of my thighs

... between my legs, stayed there a little and drove on to my breasts ..... circled around the two hills. My hands went under the shirt, pushed it a little higher and with the shout of people "down ... down" over my breasts. I went to my knees, pulled the shirt over my head, held my breasts with both hands and I turned in all directions, and finally to the boy at the St. Andrew's Cross, who was staring spellbound, and whose device had apparently already erected a little, while I massaged my breasts in front of him, twisting the warts, my eyes wandered over his body.

Slowly my hands slid deeper, stroking my stomach. I straightened up, started dancing slowly, rocking my hips. I stroked the cloth around it, enjoying my own touch. I opened it and let it fall down. The crowd went wild, the boy's gaze fixed on my triangle. I turned in a circle so that people could see me from all sides, then stopped again in front of the boy after the round. I gripped the thong with my thumb on the left and right of the belt and evenly while weighing my hips I pushed it down bit by bit over my shaved pubes. I dropped the panties, got out, danced and turned in a circle so that everyone could examine me in my nudity. I slid to my knees. Looking at the St. Andrew's Cross, I begin to stroke my breasts with one hand while the other searches for my column. I smile when I see that the boy's device is now clearly upright, licking my lips at the sight. It is certainly 17-18cm long, protrudes almost horizontally, very straight in shape, the foreskin still half over the glans and underneath, his sack hangs freely between the spread legs with the tense muscles, swings slightly.

I am now kneeling, spreading my legs, presenting him with my shame and running my hand between my thighs. Slowly I slide on my knees towards the boy. My fingers run between my labia, running them up and down. I lean back a bit to give him a better insight. When I am very close to his stiff face, I stop to enjoy the moment and the "little power" I have over the victim. The boy is sweating, his cock and his gaze clearly show that he is horny I bend down, kiss him on the feet and then up. I run my tongue up on one hand with one hand on the other side of his calves and thighs and explore his leg muscles. I too am already very hot and wet .

Hands and tongue wander along his loins, my body follows in slight serpentine lines, presses against his legs and these first touches of his body on my pubic area make me groan. My tongue and hand move on, over his taut stomach, the muscles of which are now tense, to his chest. My breast stops at the height of his limb and I slowly move my torso back and forth, enjoying the feeling of his hardness between my breasts. He sighs and I kiss him on the chest, play with his tongue on his warts. When I am completely upright, I kiss him on the neck, smell the smell of sweat that makes me wild. I press my whole body against him, hug him and pull him towards me. My foot is angled and moves back and forth between his legs. He moans louder. We both breathe hard, almost gasp.

I like to play with him, to make him horny. Slowly my head wanders deeper again, spreading kisses on his skin until I kneel in front of him directly in front of his manhood, which is now quite plump and steeply erect.

I stick my tongue out and only touch the tip of his glans, move it slightly, going to the right and left - his tail twitches, stiffens more. My two hands are between his thighs and I slowly run my fingernails up on his skin until I reach his sack. I tickle him with my fingertips. Then I take a testicle between three fingers and move it between them. In the meantime, I grabbed the root of his tail with one hand and completely pulled the foreskin back. A sigh comes from the boy's mouth. I look up, see that he has closed his eyes. He breathes violently, his chest goes up and down, he sweats .... and enjoys.

My tongue runs along the underside of the now bare glans, lets it dance on the tip of the tongue ..... a pleasure pearl comes out at the front of the glans and I run my tongue over it and lick it off. I stuck out my tongue and drove the entire length of the tail down to his sack, which I still caress with my hand. Then up again, gently nibble at the top with your teeth. The boy rears up, groans, whereupon I let my tongue circle around the glans again. He takes a deep breath when I put the tip of his tail between my lips and let my tongue circle further. When I work his tongue on the glans down with my tongue, I feel how he flinches, how his cock straightens up a bit. I enjoy this power over him

I slowly let the acorn penetrate my mouth. The boy keeps trying to jerk his pelvis to get deeper, but I always dodge my head a little. I slowly go back and forth with my lips, but I only let the stiffener slide in a little deeper. My tongue swirls around its bottom, looking for its sensitive areas. I feel him twitch under my touch and his muscles tighten and I enjoy it. He groans and rears up again and again. His hard piece continues to slide into my mouth until I have completely absorbed it. I feel his glans on my palate, start to massage it with my tongue and slowly and gently suck it. A hand tickles his balls with his fingertips, the second wanders up to his stomach. I feel his tense abs, feel it. It makes me really horny.

I slide the boy's cock out of my mouth and look up at him, grinning: "Should I finish you off now?" He just croaks and nods. My grin widened: "Then ask me for it". "Suck me out, please," he almost breathes.

Just as I want to start again, I feel like I have two hands on the pelvis and raise my butt, then push one between my wet column. A twitch goes through my body, I cry out with lust and the tied boy uses my distraction to let his pelvis snap and ram his stiff in my mouth. I swallow, then I feel the other penetrate me from behind. The hard cock in my horny column fills me up, almost takes my mind. My body twists between the two bars. Someone must have untied the boy's hands too, because he grabs my hair, holds him while he hits his pelvis hard, to finally get salvation. I gargle, suck and press my lips together, feel the tail swell in it. From the back, the rhythm is getting faster and faster. a hand has meanwhile found my clit and is massaging him mercilessly. I squirm, try to free myself, can hardly stand it, moan, scream as the boy pours into my mouth. I swallow it, soak it up. While I lose control myself and am only a twitching bundle, there is an outcry from behind and I feel how it pours warmly into me. Then I collapse, panting and whimpering. I know I have fulfilled my role as my Master. I swallow it, soak it up. While I lose control myself and am only a twitching bundle, there is an outcry from behind and I feel how it pours warmly into me. Then I collapse, panting and whimpering. I know I have fulfilled my role as my Master. I swallow it, soak it up. While I lose control myself and am only a twitching bundle, there is an outcry from behind and I feel how it pours warmly into me. Then I collapse, panting and whimpering. I know I have fulfilled my role as my Master.

The End.